Hedgehogs
from
Outer Space

By Elizabeth Morley

Published in 2015 by FeedARead.com Publishing – Arts Council funded

Copyright © text and illustrations Elizabeth Morley

First Edition

A CIP catalogue record for this title is available from the British Library.

For Monica and Ralph

Part One
Chapter One

Space. It seemed so remote as Snipper and Despina sat over coffee in their comfortable hotel in Milchnicht. The chatter of hedgehogs, the gentle music, the flickering candles - it was all so removed from the cold and vast emptiness of space.

"It's time," said Snipper, looking at his watch.

It was nine thirty-four precisely; they had three minutes to spare. Getting up from the table, the two hedgehogs wandered out into the garden and looked up into the night sky. At first they could see little, but gradually their eyes adjusted. It was a beautiful September evening. Stars twinkled in every corner of the sky; and the milky band of their galaxy stretched in a wide arc above them.

"There it is!" said Snipper, pointing. A faint speck of light had appeared high above the western horizon as though from nowhere. At first sight, it seemed indistinguishable from the stars. But, unlike them, it was moving and, as it came overhead, it grew brighter until eventually it outshone them.

"Yes, I see it now," said Despina. She still spoke with a mild foreign accent, but her fluency had been much improved by a long visit to

Snipper that summer. "How strange to think there are hedgehogs living on that tiny dot!"

The tiny dot in question was the international space station - a spacecraft the size of a football pitch, housing four laboratories, over a hundred experiments and six hedgehogs at any one time. Travelling at an extraordinary five miles a second, it orbited the Earth sixteen times a day.

"Stranger still to think Pawline will soon join them," said Snipper. Pawline was an old friend from his university days; but she had gone home to the United Stakes almost three years ago and been training as an astronaut ever since. "Strange but wonderful. I'm over the moon for her. I just wish I'd been able to show more interest in her career before now. But it's been difficult..."

"*I* know that," said Despina. "A secret agent's life can't be easy. It must make it even harder that you can't tell your friends what you really do."

"Except you, of course," said Snipper warmly. Despina was the only friend who knew his real job. They had met while working on the same secret mission - though Despina herself was no spy. She had been approached by a group of dangerous criminals, who had wanted to use her scientific expertise. While pretending to help them, she had secretly worked against them. When the mission had been accomplished and she had left the world of espionage, Snipper had been sorry to see her go. But at least now she was safe.

"It'll be nice to see Pawline again," said Despina. "And it's very kind of her friend to invite us all round before the concert."

Snipper nodded. He was looking forward to meeting Pawline's friend: Schnüffel was an experienced astronaut and would be commander of the international space station during Pawline's mission. A native of Hedgermany, he lived here in Milchnicht; and he had invited Pawline to stay so he could show her round a nearby factory that made space systems. It was purely by chance that Despina had been invited to Milchnicht the very same week. A talented amateur violinist, she had been asked to perform at the Palace Museum. This was to be her first international concert since leaving university. Snipper had flown all the way from Great Bristlin for it. He was delighted when he heard that Pawline and Schnüffel would be coming too.

And so it was that the following day Snipper, Despina and Pawline gathered together at Schnüffel's house. After an excellent Sunday

6

lunch, they relaxed in his elegant sitting room, pawing over photographs from his previous missions into space. In one of them two entire continents were visible.

"What I like about that photo," said Pawline, "is that Snipper, Despina and I are all in it even though we would have been thousands of miles apart when it was taken - each in our own country. Look - Great Bristlin, Itchaly *and* the United Stakes!"

"Will you take a camera, Pawline?" asked Snipper.

"I sure will! Everybody does. Actually, Schnüffel, wasn't there one hedgehog who preferred to sketch instead?"

"Sketch?" repeated Schnüffel, not understanding the word.

"*Skizzieren*," said Snipper helpfully.

"Oh, so you speak Hedgerman!" said Schnüffel.

"Snipper speaks every language under the sun," said Pawline. "Wherever he goes, it never takes him long to pick up the lingo. ...You know what? Perhaps we should take him with us. Then, if we come across any aliens, he can translate for us!"

The four hedgehogs laughed - none more so than Schnüffel, whose specialism was astrobiology; this included the study of the possibility of extra-terrestrial life.

"Tell me, Schnüffel," said Snipper, "joking aside, do you believe there *is* life on other planets?"

"Yes, I do. The universe is immense - there are more galaxies, solar systems and planets than you or I can imagine - so I think life must exist somewhere. Actually, some of the experiments we'll be running on the space station are to show whether micro-organisms can live and multiply in low gravity conditions - and therefore on planets considerably smaller than our own."

"What about larger and more complex organisms - creatures like us?" asked Snipper.

"Well, we'll be studying the effects on ourselves too. But that's for medical purposes. If life *does* exist on other planets, it'll be in a much less highly evolved form than us hedgehogs. So I'm afraid we probably won't be needing your language skills after all!"

"Ah well!" said Snipper, with a smile, "I'm not sure I'd be up for a trip into space anyway - it sounds a little scary!"

"But it's not like that at all!" said Pawline, who had wanted to be an astronaut ever since she had been a hoglet. "If you want something bad enough, you're so focussed on it there's no room for fear... And the training's so thorough, that any worries you have are kinda trained out of you. You know, I feel more ready for this than I have for anything else in my life."

"Pawline's right," agreed Schnüffel. "I think also it seems somehow unreal when you're down here on the ground. Even now, with two missions behind me, I'm not completely used to the idea: floating around 400 kilometres above the Earth is... Well, it's quite surprising!"

"Perhaps the music at the concert tonight will get you in the mood," said Snipper. "Despina said one of the pieces had a strange unearthly quality about it."

"In what way unearthly?" asked Schnüffel.

"I'm not sure how to explain," said Despina. "It's so different from any other music. Original and yet also very natural. It makes my spines tingle."

"Who's the composer?" asked Pawline.

"Niemandt - not that I'd ever heard of him before. It was Count de Poynte who suggested the piece - he's the music director there. Actually, when he first mentioned it, I was a little reluctant. We'd already set the programme and it meant dropping one of our other pieces. But we could hardly say no. And, once we'd played it through, we were completely won over."

"So this Count de Poynte's the music director at the Palace Museum now, is he?" asked Schnüffel. "It must be only a few months since Frau Klanger took up the post. I wonder why she left so soon."

"She hasn't left - she's ill. I'm not sure what's wrong with her but she's been off for several weeks, so they got Count de Poynte to fill in during her absence."

"I hope it's nothing serious," said Schnüffel. "But this Count de Poynte - I've not heard of him before. It's an odd name - where's he from?"

"I don't know," said Despina. "He doesn't talk much about himself, but I've been very impressed by him so far."

"Well, perhaps this will be his lucky break," said Schnüffel.

As he spoke, the doorbell rang. Despina glanced at her watch.

"That's probably my taxi," she said, rising to go. She collected her violin from the hallway. "Schnüffel, thank you *so* much for a lovely lunch. Goodbye, everyone! I'll see you all after the concert."

Little realizing just how wrong she was, Despina waved a paw and, without a backward glance, left.

Chapter Two

"Pretty cool, huh?" said Pawline, when the first half of the concert was over. "But did you see those hedgehogs just behind us? So *rude*! I can't understand why anyone would walk out in the middle of such a beautiful piece. But never mind them. Don't you agree Despina's solo passage was just awesome?"

"Your friend's extremely talented," observed Schnüffel. "I'm surprised she hasn't made a career in music."

"Oh, the violin's just one of Despina's many talents," said Snipper. "Shall we get those drinks I ordered? The interval's only fifteen minutes."

Getting up from their seats, the three hedgehogs proceeded outside to the courtyard, where a table had been set up for refreshments. They helped themselves to a glass each of the famous local beer.

"So what *does* Despina do for a living?" asked Schnüffel. "I imagine it must be something special - to keep her from music."

"It is," said Snipper. "She's a hydrologist - a water expert. At the moment she's working on some flood defences for her home town. As you can imagine, the project means a great deal to her. But, once that's over, I suppose she might switch careers."

"You think so?" asked Pawline. "You reckon she'll become a professional violinist?"

"It's certainly one possibility," said Snipper.

"That would be amazing!" said Pawline enthusiastically. "She might become a big star and get invited all over the world. Then she could come visit me in the United Stakes. Mind you, I hope you'll *both* be coming over much sooner than that, for the space launch. You *will* make it, won't you, Snipper?" she asked doubtfully.

"Actually, I've already booked my flight."

"You're kidding me!" exclaimed Pawline. "That's fantastic! I really didn't think you'd come."

"I wouldn't miss it for the world," said Snipper, but he regretted the words as soon as they were spoken. For he frequently had to drop everything to go on some mission or other. Sometimes that meant letting his friends down, but there was nothing he could do about that: his job would always have to come first. "So," he said, brushing aside these niggling doubts, "will I get to see this giant magnet you'll be looking after?"

"You mean the alpha magnetic spectrometer? No, it's already up there. But I'll be doing a space walk to assess its condition, and you'll be able to check out my photos online afterwards. You know, it's a real exciting project. That 'magnet' is gonna help us find all kinds of unusual matter - anti-matter, strange matter, maybe even dark matter..."

Pawline started explaining all about matter to her friends. But it was a complicated subject and she was still explaining when the bell rang, summoning them back to the concert hall. Settling back into their seats, they waited keenly for the performers to appear. But ten minutes passed and there was still no sign of them. Instead, a solitary hedgehog in black tie emerged from a side door. Raising a paw, he signalled the audience to be silent.

"*Meine Damen und Herren,*" he said gravely, "*Ich bedaure, Ihnen mitteilen zu müssen, dass Fräulein Despina...*"

"Hey Schnüffel, what's he saying?" whispered Pawline.

"He regrets that Fräulein Despina... My goodness, he says she's been taken ill!"

"Ill?" frowned Pawline. "So suddenly?"

"I'll go and see what the matter is," said Snipper, who had already risen from his seat. "You two stay here and enjoy the rest of the concert."

Snipper slipped out the back, just as the other performers appeared. Marching smartly to Despina's dressing room, he knocked loudly on

her door but there was no answer. He let himself in. She was not there, but her bag was on the dressing table and her violin was on the floor; next to it, lay her bow - snapped clean in two. A shiver ran down Snipper's spines. Despina's abandoned bag, her precious violin lying on the floor and the broken bow could surely mean only one thing: there had been a struggle - Despina had not left this room willingly.

Snipper ran out of the room and hurried off in the direction of the street. There was no sign of Despina. He tried ringing her mobile but there was no answer so he turned back. As he reached her dressing room, he could hear her familiar ring-tone coming from inside her bag, so he rang off. For a moment he hesitated, wondering whether to search her bag. The secret agent within him wanted to look for clues. But he had no wish to contaminate the scene of a crime with his pawprints. So he left her bag where it was.

If only he could think of a possible motive, he would have something to go on. But why would anyone come after Despina? Back in the spring, when she had been working under cover, she had made some dangerous enemies, but the mission was over now. She had gone back to her regular job. And the criminals were all behind bars - all but one and, only yesterday, *he* had been traced to Hogotà, on the far side of the world.

Snipper was getting nowhere, so he decided to call the police. But, before he could do so, a sound behind him made him spin round. A hedgehog was standing in the doorway clutching a musical score in his paws. It was the hedgehog who had made the announcement that Despina was too unwell to perform.

"Where's Despina?" asked Snipper suspiciously, in perfect Hedgerman. "And who are you?"

"*I* should be asking that question," said the other hedgehog. Snipper noticed he spoke with a faint foreign accent. It had a sing-song quality to it but he could not place it. "I'm Count de Poynte, the music director here, but I've not seen *you* before."

"My name's Snipper, and I'm a friend of Despina, who *you* said was ill..."

"Yes, I'm afraid she isn't at all well. She became dizzy and feverish, so I sent her back to the hotel in a taxi. Still, after a good night's sleep…"

"You put her in a taxi, did you? Then perhaps you'd like to explain why her bag's still here, her violin's on the floor and her bow's been snapped in two."

"Goodness me!" exclaimed de Poynte, who looked as though he were noticing these things for the first time. "She must have dropped them - she really *was* in a bad way. She'll be extremely upset when she realizes. Perhaps you could take them to her - I'm sure she'd like to see a friendly face."

"No doubt," said Snipper frostily. "But I think I should speak to her first, don't you? In fact, I'll call the hotel right now, then we can both speak to her."

"Oh, I hardly think that's necessary..."

"Perhaps you'd rather I call the police," said Snipper sharply.

"The police! What an extraordinary suggestion! Why would you want to bring them into this?"

"Either that or you tell me what you've done with her."

De Poynte frowned. But he was either unwilling or unable to defend himself, for he made no reply.

"Come on, out with it!" insisted Snipper. "You've got one minute before I call the police - with or without your version of events."

"All right, I'll tell you," said de Poynte at last. "I didn't before because the truth is too... Well, you see, Despina's been kidnapped."

"*That* much I'd already worked out for myself," said Snipper impatiently. "What I want to know is where you've taken her and why."

"*I've* not taken her anywhere. But I'm afraid you must prepare yourself for a shock - an even bigger shock, that is."

"Yes?" pressed Snipper anxiously.

"You may find it difficult to believe."

"For pity's sake, just tell me the truth!" pleaded Snipper.

"Despina's been kidnapped by hedgehogs from outer space."

Snipper stared at de Poynte in astonishment and then spoke with barely concealed anger: "What kind of a sick joke is that?"

"It wasn't a joke. I was speaking the truth."

Snipper made no reply but, without further ado, called the police. There was no time to be lost in finding Despina, and he was not going to waste another second questioning de Poynte, who appeared to be criminally insane. As he punched in the emergency number, he fixed de Poynte with an icy stare, half expecting him to make a dash for the door or grab the phone off him. But de Poynte stayed where he was, apparently deep in thought.

"Police," said Snipper. "Yes, I want to report a kidnapping... That's right... From the Palace Museum within the last half hour... My name's Snipper. I'm a friend... Yes, I'll be here - and there's someone else you should to speak to. His name's Count de Poynte. He's the music director here... Yes, all right. Thanks. Bye." Ringing off, Snipper now addressed de Poynte. "Well, what do you say to that? The police are already on their way. If you repeat your nonsense to *them*, you'll be arrested for wasting police time."

"Then it'll have to be our little secret," said de Poynte. "In any case, the police can do nothing for Despina. By now she's well beyond their reach - and beyond the reach of any Earthling."

Hearing de Poynte persist with his ridiculous story made Snipper want to storm out of the room. But instead he now played along: he was determined not to let him out of his sight before the police arrived.

"All right then," he said. "Let's assume Despina's no longer on Earth. I'd still like to know where she is – and I'm sure you're dying to tell me."

"I imagine they're taking her back to their planet. It's called Verdis."

"And how do you know it was these hedgehogs from Verdis that took her?"

"I saw them - a group of Verdissians carrying her out of the room. She was unconscious, so I assume they must have drugged her. I did try and stop them but I was outnumbered; they overpowered me."

"I see," said Snipper coldly. "And what was it about them that made you think they were Verdissians?"

"I don't think - I *know*," said de Poynte. He spoke emphatically but then hesitated before continuing: "You see… the thing is… I myself am from outer space."

"You?" said Snipper, suppressing an urge to smile in spite of everything. "You're a Verdissian, are you?"

"Certainly not!" exclaimed de Poynte. "I'm from Cerulea. We're their neighbours but nothing like the Verdissians. We're explorers - not pirates. I'm here to study Earthling culture and history. In fact, I'm under orders to neither interfere nor even let my presence be known. That's why I was reluctant to tell you the truth."

For a moment, Snipper simply stared at de Poynte. His persistence with such an absurd story was almost as unbelievable as the story itself.

"Enough!" he said bristling with fury as he finally let out his pent-up feelings. "Enough of this drivel! You stand there - no different to me or any other hedgehog on Earth - and expect me - you *really* expect me to believe you're from outer space! What kind of an idiot do you take me for?"

"You've perhaps not heard of convergent evolution," said de Poynte. "Your species and mine have evolved along parallel lines. We may look similar but, if you test my DNA, you'll find appearances can be deceptive. Furthermore, to appear truly like an Earthling, we must drink a special chemical solution which changes our natural blue to brown."

"Oh, so you're really *blue!*" said Snipper scornfully. "I suppose you're going to tell me the Verdissians are green."

"Well, yes - as a matter of fact, they are."

"Then prove it!"

"Very well, I will. But you'll need to be patient. You see, the effects wear off only gradually. And, of course, once I'm back to my natural blue, I can't be seen in public. But, if you give me your contact details, I'll send you a message - telling you where and when to meet me. Then you'll know I've been telling the truth."

Snipper hesitated. He suspected de Poynte was simply trying to get rid of him; and he did not much like the idea of giving him his contact details. But neither could he just walk away. "What about Despina in the meantime?" he asked. "You must be out of your mind if you think I'm just going to sit on my paws, waiting for a message from you."

"How you choose to spend your time is your own business," said de Poynte, with a shrug of his shoulders. "But it'll make no difference to Despina. You cannot reach her now."

"So you said. But why can't you tell me now when and where I'm to meet you?"

"Why should I?" asked de Poynte; it was clear he would not budge.

Snipper finally relented and gave de Poynte his mobile number and hotel address. As de Poynte was entering these details on his phone, he suddenly pricked up his ears. Indeed, they had both heard the same thing – police sirens, followed by a screech of brakes and slamming of car doors out in the courtyard. On hearing this, de Poynte promptly turned tail and left. Snipper dashed after him but then stopped when he saw that de Poynte had walked straight into the police.

Snipper had not been spotted. With his head still reeling, he returned to Despina's dressing room; he needed a few minutes to himself to collect his thoughts before speaking to the police. Sinking down onto Despina's dressing stool, he replayed his conversation with de Poynte over and over again in his head. What was de Poynte playing at? What possible motive could he have for kidnapping Despina? And why try to explain away the lies about an illness with an absurd story nobody was going to believe? As for meeting de Poynte at some secret location, Snipper was convinced that it was either a trap or else de

Poynte had no real intention of turning up. Yet Snipper felt he had to go, if there was just the smallest chance of finding Despina.

"Snipper! What's happened? Why are the police here?" It was Pawline, who had suddenly appeared with Schnüffel. They had left the concert early when Snipper had failed to return. "Where's Despina? Is she all right?"

"She's gone," said Snipper. "She's been kidnapped."

"Kidnapped!" exclaimed Pawline incredulously. Then she noticed the violin and the broken bow on the floor. "Why on earth would anyone...?"

"So did *you* call the police?" asked Schnüffel.

Snipper nodded. "Look, I'm going to see if I can find a security guard. They may have seen something. Better still, they may have caught something on CCTV. Pawline, you'd better come with me. You might recognize those hedgehogs who walked out during the first half of the concert."

"I don't know," responded Pawline, hesitantly. "I only saw the backs of their heads, but I guess I might recognize their clothes."

"Hold on, you two!" said Schnüffel. "The police won't like it if they find out you've started your own private investigation."

"Never mind what the police would like," said Snipper, a little rudely. "What *I* would like is to find Despina."

So saying, he went off with Pawline. They quickly found a security guard and together scanned all the CCTV footage, covering every exit over the last half hour. Yet there was no sign of either Despina or the hedgehogs who had left early. Schnüffel, meanwhile, was left to deal with the police. The officer in charge was understandably annoyed to find that Snipper had wandered off. Schnüffel covered for him, saying he must have got lost while searching for Despina - the corridors of the Palace Museum were certainly maze-like. Then the head of security turned up, following a call from one of his guards. The police and guards, between them, set about planning a thorough search of the premises and sent another unit off to check Despina's hotel. The search had just begun when Snipper reappeared, apologising profusely.

"Please, come this way, Herr Snipper," said a police officer with a notepad. He beckoned him into one of several makeshift interview rooms. "I'm sorry to make this so formal, but I'm sure you understand that we have certain procedures we must follow."

"Of course," said Snipper. "And I want to do everything I can to help. Despina's my friend."

"Just so," said the police officer. "Now, I must first take a few personal details. Starting with your full name and address. Also your occupation."

Snipper produced a business card describing him as an 'art dealer'. He preferred to keep his real occupation to himself, but the name and address on the card were correct.

"Are you here on business or for pleasure?"

"Pleasure. I came to hear Despina play in the concert."

"What about your friends, Herr Schnüffel and Fräulein Pawline?"

"Aren't you going to ask *them*?"

"Certainly. But we'd also like to hear from you... in your own words."

"Very well then," said Snipper, "Schnüffel lives in Milchnicht and Pawline's here on business, staying with him. They're going round the Astellaritz space factory tomorrow. It was just chance that Despina was performing in a concert here tonight."

"So that's Schnüffel the famous astronaut, is it?" asked the officer, looking a little awestruck. "I thought I recognized him! Well, his face *has* been all over the TV and newspapers lately. He'll be Hedgermany's first ever commander of the international space station."

"So I gather," said Snipper. He was well aware of the fact that Schnüffel had renewed his country's interest in all things space-related.

For a moment he wondered whether de Poynte had simply been swept away with space-fever and lost his grip on reality.

"So how long have you known Fräulein Despina?" asked the officer.

"We met on holiday last February, so... seven months."

"Just seven months, you say? Yet you flew all the way from Great Bristlin to Hedgermany to hear her play the violin?"

"Well, we hit it off," said Snipper vaguely. He was reluctant to say that he felt closer to Despina than to any other hedgehog he knew. How could the officer possibly understand without knowing what they had been through together? "Besides," he added, "she's an extremely gifted violinist."

There was a moment's silence while the officer scribbled in his notebook. "Now," he said, looking up again, "I'd like you to tell me about the events of this evening - starting from when you last saw Despina. Please omit nothing."

"Well, I last *saw* her when she was playing the violin during the first half of the concert. But I also met her before the concert - we all did..." Snipper duly told the police officer everything. He told him about the hedgehogs Pawline had spotted leaving the concert early. And he told him about de Poynte and the absurd story he had spun.

20

"I see," said the officer. A hint of a smile passed over his face as he spoke. "Well, Count de Poynte is being interviewed right now so we shall hear his own version of events directly."

"He won't tell you the same story," said Snipper. "He said so himself. But, you know, I've been trying to think why he would have cooked up such a ridiculous story for *me*. I was hardly likely to believe it. I think he must be playing some sort of sick game. I don't know what motive he could possibly have, but I'd bet anything he's involved in the kidnapping. As for that message he says he'll send me - "

"Please don't worry about that, sir. If this business hasn't been sorted out by then, just forward the message to us and we'll take it from there. In the meantime, I think we need to examine this problem from the other end. Can you think of any reason why someone would kidnap Despina?"

"None at all."

"Does she come from a rich family?"

"No. I believe they live comfortably, but I wouldn't describe them as rich."

"Does she have any enemies?"

Snipper considered the question for a moment. The criminals she had helped bring to justice were no longer a threat. Besides, the case was Top Secret, and he did not have permission to talk about it. "No," he said, "she has no enemies that I know of."

"I see," said the officer. "So you can think of no motive? Would you describe Despina as a happy hedgehog?"

"Yes, I would," said Snipper, who did not like the direction the interview was now taking.

"She has no personal problems that you're aware of?"

"No," said Snipper, "and, if you're suggesting she ran off, of her own accord and in the middle of an important concert - leaving her bag, her violin and a mysteriously broken bow behind... Well, then you're very much mistaken."

Chapter Three

By the time Snipper got back to his hotel, it was past ten o'clock and he decided to go straight to bed. But sleep was impossible. As a secret agent he had been through many a dark hour before, when danger had lurked around every corner and more than one hedgehog's life had been at risk. Yet this was different. Despina was his closest friend. He would have been out there right now, tramping the city streets, had he thought it would do any good. But she might just as well have disappeared in a puff of smoke.

Snipper now feared he had been wrong to tell the police about the promised message from de Poynte. The police would probably try to prevent him from keeping his appointment and go to the rendez-vous themselves. What if they blundered in on the place where Despina's captors were holding her? What would happen to his friend then? Snipper got out of bed and started to pace up and down. He wanted to know more about this hedgehog de Poynte. Where did he come from? Who were his associates? It was time to do a little research. Getting up early the following morning, Snipper straightaway rang the Palace Museum.

"Palace Museum Events Office," said a female voice. "How can I help you?"

"Ah, good morning," said Snipper. "I've a meeting with Count de Poynte at his office today. I wonder if you could give me directions. The Palace Museum's such a big place, I fear I may get lost."

"May I enquire what the meeting's about, sir? Only Count de Poynte is leaving us today. If you're seeing him in connection with an event at the Palace Museum, you'll need to arrange a new appointment with Frau Klanger."

"No, it's a private matter," said Snipper. "It's Count de Poynte I want to see. He hasn't gone yet, has he?"

"No, he should be here until four o'clock. What time is your meeting?"

"Oh, that'll be fine," said Snipper. "So the entrance I need is...?"

"The west gate, opposite the church. Then just follow the signs. Is there anything else I can help you with, sir?"

"No, you've been most helpful already, thanks." Snipper rang off quickly before the receptionist could ask any more questions.

So Count de Poynte was leaving today - the very day after Despina's disappearance. On the face of it, the timing had been determined by

Frau Klanger's return to work, not by Despina's abduction. Yet Snipper felt certain there *was* a connection with his friend's disappearance. Throwing on his jacket, he headed straight over to the Palace Museum's west gate.

From a surveillance point of view, this was quite an exposed spot. The street was surprisingly empty, with just a solitary hedgehog walking briskly along, clutching a briefcase. But just around the corner Snipper noticed a number of hedgehogs gathered on some steps with a good view of the exit. They were dressed in national costume and clearly here for the city's autumn folk festival. As they seemed in no hurry to move, Snipper went and sat among them, carefully choosing a spot behind a pillar. Then he waited.

At twenty past twelve, his patience was rewarded, for de Poynte had appeared. Snipper made a mental note of his clothes. Then, just as de Poynte was disappearing from view, Snipper jumped to his feet and set off in pursuit. A minute later, he caught sight of him again and slowed down. Continuing at a steady pace now, Snipper carefully maintained his distance until they reached the town square. This was a popular tourist site, bristling with hedgehogs. Here the likelihood of being spotted reduced, but the likelihood of losing de Poynte grew. Snipper sped up, closing the gap between them until they were just a few feet apart. The two hedgehogs turned right across the crowded square and passed through the city gate. Here de Poynte paused; Snipper did likewise. Pretending to check his phone for messages, Snipper watched de Poynte out of the corner of his eye, as he first glanced at his watch and then entered a restaurant. Snipper waited one minute and then followed him in.

The restaurant was much larger on the inside than it had appeared from the street, and extremely busy. Beneath its low-vaulted ceiling, waiters and waitresses negotiated their way skilfully between the tables, clutching platefuls of *würst* and other local specialities. The customers were a mixed crowd - office workers on their lunch break, the usual tourists and quite a few hedgehogs in national costume, who had come for the festival.

Count de Poynte was seated in a far corner of the room. With him were two other hedgehogs, whom Snipper had not seen before. Snipper considered for a moment where to sit in order to get the best view. There were two empty tables nearby. One was right next to de Poynte and his companions, but Snipper would certainly have been spotted there. The other, though further off, had a good view and was out of de Poynte's direct line of sight. It would probably do just as well as the first: proximity was certainly no guarantee of overhearing the conversation above the general hubbub. As Snipper made his way over to his chosen table, he was intercepted by a helpful waitress. She recommended a place at the front of the restaurant, next to the window. Snipper declined politely but firmly. On taking his seat, he ordered himself a hearty meal, although he did not feel the slightest bit hungry. The ability to stoke up on food was a trick he had learnt as a secret agent - a sensible precaution in case he found himself on the go for hours on end.

When the waitress had gone, Snipper got out his phone and pretended to make a call. He said a few words. Then he made a show of listening - nodding or smiling every now and then, with the occasional *"ja"* or *"nein"* thrown in. In reality, however, his attention was focussed firmly on de Poynte's table. Though he was out of earshot, Snipper was a good lip-reader and now hoped to learn exactly what this meeting was about.

For the first few minutes, de Poynte did most of the talking and, because he had his back to Snipper, there was naturally no possibility of lip-reading. But, when the others did speak, Snipper could make neither head nor tail of it. Their speech bore no resemblance to anything he had ever come across before - though he was fluent in eight languages and had more than a passing knowledge of many more. Frustrated by this turn of events, he was nevertheless not one to throw away an opportunity. Tucking into his lunch, he concentrated instead on examining the appearance and behaviour of these three hedgehogs.

25

Perhaps the most striking thing about them was that, while de Poynte himself wore a blazer and tie, his companions were dressed quite casually. The taller of the two wore a denim jacket, cotton trousers and deck shoes. The other, who was a little on the tubby side, wore a jumper, jeans and trainers. Snipper also noticed a streak of fresh mud on the latter's shoes; and he thought they both looked a little wind-swept. Yet there had not been even a hint of a breeze in Milchnicht this morning, and he remembered Schnüffel saying it had not rained for a week. Perhaps they had travelled in from the country. Whatever the case, this did not look like a social visit, for their manner was businesslike and very respectful. Indeed, Snipper had the distinct impression that de Poynte was in charge.

Here, however, his observations ended. And, since there was little more to be deduced from this scene, he began to wish they would eat up and depart. But they seemed in no hurry to leave. Then, just after they had started on their pudding, a family group came in and took the table next to them. When the tall hedgehog saw them, he put his paw on his companion's arm to silence him.

"Ssh! We aren't alone!" he said, in what Snipper assumed must be a whisper. Suddenly Snipper was able to lip-read every word.

The tall hedgehog had spoken in Hedgerman. Why? Snipper could not understand his decision to switch languages. There was little

chance of being overheard above the general noise. But, if they *were* afraid of this, then surely that was all the more reason to stick to their own language.

"Well, sir, we've got our passes now," said the tall hedgehog, apparently in response to a question from de Poynte. "They're as good as the real thing. We've already put them to the test and got into the factory without any problems. No one challenged us. But the interior layout isn't what we expected. The item we're after is in a sealed off area. There's a whole extra layer of security surrounding it, which we're going to have to get through."

Snipper was astonished. De Poynte was planning to break into a factory - a high security factory, by the sound of it.

"Of course," continued the tall hedgehog, "their security arrangements aren't sophisticated by our standards. The trouble is we're not equipped to deal with old technology."

De Poynte spoke next. Judging by the others' unhappy expressions, he was not very impressed by these excuses.

"Yes, sir," responded the tall hedgehog. "We'll definitely have cracked it by tomorrow."

De Poynte spoke again.

"Well, sir," said the tubby hedgehog, "we'll easily have enough fuel by Friday. And, if we leave the pumps on in the day, we can be ready earlier than that."

De Poynte nodded and at last appeared satisfied, for here the conversation ended. The three hedgehogs now finished their meal in silence, leaving Snipper to reflect on what he had heard and see if he could make any sense of it.

There had been no clues as to the factory's location. The item they intended to steal was a single item, and the extra layer of security suggested it was dangerous, valuable or both. But the security had also been described as unsophisticated and out-of-date, which suggested an old factory which had failed to keep up with the times. The day of the break-in was a little clearer - some time this week, Friday at the latest but probably earlier. As for the sudden switch of languages halfway through the conversation, had they perhaps *wanted* to be overheard? Snipper did not believe it. But what other explanation could there be? Most confusingly of all, it was impossible to see any connection between the burglary and Despina's abduction.

Snipper's reflections now came to an end, for the three hedgehogs had asked for their bill. Chances were they would part company once more. So who should Snipper follow now? De Poynte was the leader of the group but he would surely just head back to the Palace Museum, where he was not expected to finish until four. The others, however, were busy preparing for the factory break-in. On the face of it, the break-in was a distraction from the all-important task of finding Despina. But instinct told Snipper otherwise. Over his years as a secret agent, he had learned that the criminal underworld operated according to a strict set of rules; one of these was that a criminal gang should never stray into another gang's patch. So, when two major crimes occurred in one area over the course of just one week, they were almost certain to be connected.

Snipper made his decision just as the three got up to leave the restaurant. Out in the street, when they parted as he had expected, he let de Poynte return to the Palace Museum alone and instead followed his two henchhogs. No longer fearing to be recognized, Snipper walked just a few feet behind them as they made their way westwards. On reaching the ring road surrounding the old city centre, the two hedgehogs stopped and looked around, as though seeking someone or something. A black saloon car on the far side of the road tooted and pulled over alongside them. Snipper quickly hailed a taxi.

"Where to?" asked the driver, as Snipper tumbled into the back seat.

"Follow that car!" said Snipper, indicating the black saloon.

The driver looked startled for a moment, then grinned delightedly and put his foot down on the pedal. They were off.

"After all these years!" exclaimed the driver. "Twenty years of driving! Who'd have thought it? I've had some funny requests in my time, mind you. Hedgehogs who've wanted me to drive round and round in circles... And one who wanted me to take him all the way to Igelstadt. That's 70 kilometres, you know - without the corners! But *follow that car*! Well, I thought that was just in films... So," he said, glancing in his mirror as he weaved skilfully through the lunchtime traffic, "you're some sort of spook, are you?"

"No," lied Snipper. "I'm just trying to find a friend who's disappeared."

"Oh, I see," said the driver, suddenly looking sombre. "You think the hedgehogs in the car ahead are involved, do you?"

"Yes," said Snipper. "Well, I'm not sure... but I can't sit around doing nothing about it."

"No, I suppose that's a job for the police!" said the driver, smiling at his own joke. Then he remembered himself and looked sombre again. "I'm sorry sir... But don't you worry - I won't let them out of my sight."

The black car now turned right and headed south. Before long, they had left the city behind and were in a delightfully tidy landscape of rolling green fields, onion-topped churches and pretty wooden houses bedecked with flowers. In the far distance, the faint silhouette of the Altispine Mountains stretched across the horizon like a low-hanging cloud.

There was little conversation. The taxi driver could see Snipper did not want to talk about his friend's disappearance, and idle chit-chat seemed inappropriate. For his own part, Snipper kept his eyes on the car in front, fearing that at any moment it would speed ahead or turn off without warning. But, if the occupants knew they were being followed, they gave no indication of it.

It was only about thirty minutes later, as they were approaching the Altispine Mountains, that the taxi driver finally broke his silence: "Sir, I'm afraid my fuel light's come on. I won't be able to follow if they go much further."

"How much further do you think you can manage?" asked Snipper.

"At this speed, 20 kilometres."

"Well, they can't be going very much further, can they?" asked Snipper anxiously, as though the taxi driver could have any better idea of where they were going.

"I don't know, sir. There's not much out here, except the lake and a few farming villages. Perhaps they're heading for the border."

But, just as he finished speaking, the black car turned off towards the lake. Why on earth, wondered Snipper, would they be heading here? Surely they had a factory to burgle! Yet again nothing seemed to make any sense. But at least it looked as though the fuel would last the journey after all.

A few minutes later, they arrived at a ferry terminal serving a group of islands at the southern end of the lake. De Poynte's two henchhogs got out of their car and wandered off towards the quay. They seemed in no hurry. Snipper hesitated for a moment, wondering whether to follow them or stay with the black car. But their driver had only been waiting for a parking place. As soon as she had got one, she jumped out and made her way to the ticket kiosk. Snipper quickly paid his fare and followed her. Joining the queue just behind her, he pricked up his ears as she asked for three tickets to Igelininsel. Snipper bought his own ticket and proceeded directly to the quay, where he spotted all three hedgehogs in the process of boarding.

Following them up onto the sun deck, he found a seat right next to them. But, frustratingly, they sat in silence, gazing out at the view as the ferry set off towards the middle of the lake. The scenery was certainly very fine. The three islands lay clustered together a little way out from the shore. They were all low-lying and heavily wooded; and, though the trees were still green, there was a touch of red and gold about them which hinted at autumn. On the lake numerous colourful dinghies and sleek yachts glided past, along with the occasional no-nonsense fishing boat. And looming dramatically over this friendly scene were the Altispine Mountains.

As they approached Igelininsel, it became clear there were quite a few buildings dotted among the trees. At the near end of the island was a handsome convent with an onion-topped church. Further along, the shore was lined with pretty houses, each with its own jetty or miniature harbour and a garden leading down to the water's edge.

Snipper disembarked just behind his three companions. A short walk took them round to the far side of the island, where they let themselves into a large white house decorated with window boxes full of red geraniums. Pausing as though to admire the view, Snipper examined the house out of the corner of his eye. Its shutters were all open, there was no sign of a net curtain in any of the windows and the garden was in full view of the public footpath. If Despina was being held captive

31

here, it was a strange place to choose - with neighbours on both sides and holiday-makers walking past the front door. Then again, neither was it an obvious spot from which to mastermind a factory break-in - and of that, at least, Snipper was more certain.

Snipper wondered whether they intended to transport the stolen goods here and, if so, how. They would surely not dare take anything too big or conspicuous onto the ferry. Perhaps they had their own boat. Just across the path was a boathouse adorned with more red geraniums. It obviously formed part of the same property. Snipper noticed there were blinds pulled down inside, preventing anyone from looking in - and he had never seen blinds in a boathouse before.

He glanced up at the house. There was no sign of anyone looking out. But it would be better all the same to have some sort of cover. So he waited. Before long a large party of tourists appeared on the path, coming the other way. Snipper noted with satisfaction that they were ambling, in the manner of all large groups. Making his way slowly towards them, he made sure he reached the house just as they did. Then, as soon as he was shielded from view by the crowd, he left the path and grabbed the handle of the boathouse door. But it was locked. He glanced back. The tourists were moving on now, but a small group had stayed behind to admire the flowers.

Quick as a flash, Snipper slipped round the back, out of sight of the main house. At first glance, this approach appeared no better. The lakeside entrance, through which a boat would enter, was shuttered; and there was no way of opening it from the outside. It was going to be difficult getting into the boathouse without drawing attention to himself, unless under cover of darkness. Snipper checked his watch: it was only three o'clock in the afternoon and would not be dark for over four hours. He considered waiting. His training as a secret agent had taught him the virtue of patience. But what if Despina was here? Anything could happen in four hours. Was he really just going to sit here doing nothing?

Throwing caution to the wind, Snipper glanced round to check no one was looking, then removed his jacket and shoes, and dropped into the lake. Though the water was murky with algae and mud, Snipper kept below the surface. Switching on the torch in his special-issue Secret Service watch, he could just make out the stone walls beneath the boathouse. Between them, the pulled-down shutter came to within an inch of the water but no further: underwater, the entrance was wide open. Snipper swam through. Surfacing on the inside, he wiped the algae from his face and surveyed the scene.

It was not at all what he had expected. There was neither boat nor boating equipment, just a row of machines. Then, as Snipper swam over to get a better look, the light came on. Startled, he ducked under the water, swivelling round to see who had come through the door. But there was no one there: clearly his own movement must have triggered a sensor.

Snipper broke surface and resumed his examination. There was a pipe coming out of the water. This was connected to a couple of purification tanks, a large industrial freezer and a giant mixer. It looked as though water was being extracted from the lake, then purified, frozen, mixed with some other substance, and finally packed into small blue cylinders. Snipper remembered the conversation back in the restaurant. They had mentioned pumps and fuel. But what kind of fuel used frozen water? And what on earth was it for? The more he learned, the less he seemed to understand. But, whatever the answer, it was clear they needed an awful lot of the stuff, for on the opposite walkway were stacks of the blue cylinders - about thirty or forty of them in all.

A little shiver ran down Snipper's spines, reminding him it was almost October and no time to remain wet for long. He knew he had

been reckless diving into the water, for he could hardly walk around in wet clothes without drawing attention to himself. But it looked as though he was in luck. Pulling himself out of the water, he went over to the freezer and held a paw over the vent at the back. A steady stream of hot air was coming out - just as with a kitchen freezer, only a great deal warmer. Squeezing behind it, Snipper placed himself in the stream of hot air.

When Snipper's clothes were no longer visibly wet, he turned his attention to the blue cylinders. For a moment he wondered if he should try opening one. But who knew what dangerous substance he might release? So he settled for caution and merely photographed the cylinders and the machinery. Then, as there was nothing more to see, he decided it was time to leave.

Getting out looked a lot simpler than getting in, as the lakeside shutter was operated from inside. At the press of a button, the shutter began to rise. But it was only about halfway up, when Snipper heard footsteps outside the door. There was no time to be lost. Pulling his shirt sleeve over his paw, he quickly loosened the hot light bulb, for this was the only way of turning it off. Then he sent the shutter into reverse. But now he could hear the sound of a key being inserted in the lock. Bending forwards, he leapt out beneath the descending shutter. He landed on the grass a couple of inches from the water's edge.

Steadying himself, he looked back to see the shutter was now down. But had he been heard? As he put on his shoes and jacket, he kept his ear to the wall. He could hear voices. Bizarrely, it sounded as though they were singing - not talking. More importantly, however, there were three of them. That meant there was a good chance the house was empty. Seizing his opportunity, he rushed up to the front door and, finding it unlocked, let himself in.

There were three rooms on the ground floor. In the sitting room, a local newspaper lay on the coffee table, alongside a collection of dirty mugs. Otherwise there was little sign of activity and nothing of interest. Next along was the dining room. On the table was what looked like the remains of breakfast, lunch and supper. Snipper noticed there were crumbs on the floor and the place did not look as though it had been dusted for a while. In the kitchen, the draining board was covered in piles of dirty crockery, and the cooker smeared with burnt-on food. But there was no sign of Despina anywhere, or of anything to connect her with the occupants of the house. And upstairs was no different.

A wave of disappointment swept over Snipper. What had he been thinking? What was he even doing here? The only link between this place and Despina was de Poynte's lunch meeting with the hedgehogs living here. Furthermore, there was no real evidence that de Poynte, himself, had been involved in the kidnapping. No normal kidnapper would draw attention to himself by relaying such a stupid story. Yet there was nothing about de Poynte's looks or manner to suggest he was mad. And, if not mad, he had to have a reason for inventing such nonsense.

So Snipper did not go just yet. Though his friend was not here, a more thorough search might at least reveal some sort of clue to her whereabouts. There were still chests-of-drawers to check and a study desk piled high with papers. Returning to the study, he sat down at the desk and worked his way through the papers, one by one.

The first two items were a couple of unpaid bills. The next was a flyer for Despina's concert - not particularly surprising given de Poynte was the musical director for the event. But beneath the flyer was an intriguing brown envelope. As Snipper emptied the contents out onto the desk, his jaw dropped. Two very new-looking identity cards lay before him. Made out in the names of Stern and Schnuppe, their photographs showed de Poynte's two lunchtime companions. But it was the company name on the cards that made Snipper gape in astonishment. It was none other than Astellaritz, the space factory which Pawline and Schnüffel were visiting today.

Snipper felt sure the identity cards were fakes and Astellaritz was the factory they intended to burgle. He wondered whether de Poynte was interested in Pawline and Schnüffel as well as Despina, though they would be long gone before the burglary took place. And there was one other thing about the factory which stood out. Astellaritz specialized in satellites, rockets and space robotics. Snipper could hardly ignore the connection with de Poynte's claim to be from outer space. Astellaritz made just the sort of things a space traveller might want to steal. Perhaps de Poynte really did believe himself to be some sort of alien and was after spare parts for his imaginary spaceship. But there were three other hedgehogs involved in this and surely they could not all be mad... Had de Poynte actually been telling the truth?

ASTELLARITZ

Nahme: Stern
Stellung: Ingenieur
Unterschrift: Stern
Ausweisnummer: F14982

Diese Ausweis gohört auf Astellaritz
Diese Ausweis gohört auf Astellaritz

Brushing these absurd thoughts aside, Snipper returned the identity cards to their envelope and resumed his search. As he went through the desk drawers, his eye was caught by a plain metallic cylinder with a single button on one side. He placed it on the desk and pressed the button. A holographic projection of the Earth appeared. Though he had seen holograms before, this looked so real he instinctively leant forward to touch it with his paw. To his astonishment, it felt completely solid. He touched it again, and this time place names

36

appeared. Now he tried brushing the hologram with his paw and found he could make the globe spin on its axis. Spinning it round to Hedgermany, he spotted three dots marking Milchnicht, Astellaritz and Igelininsel: the city where Despina had been kidnapped, the space factory which was about to be burgled and this island. A fourth unmarked dot lay on the equator - adrift in the middle of the ocean. He tapped the dot marking Astellaritz, whereupon the globe vanished; it was now replaced by another projection of a large industrial building, its grounds and immediate surroundings.

Snipper watched, fascinated, as tiny life-like trees swayed in an invisible breeze and two even tinier hedgehogs swiped their ID cards at the main gate and then made their way up to the front entrance. Just as they disappeared into the building, the sound of footsteps on the staircase made Snipper jump up. Turning off the hologram, he slipped the projector into his pocket with the ID cards and looked for a place to hide. But, before he could move, the tall hedgehog in the denim jacket had appeared in the doorway.

"Who are you? What are you doing in here?" he asked sharply. Snipper noticed he spoke Hedgerman with the same unplaceable sing-song accent as Count de Poynte.

"My name's Snipper. I'm looking for Despina."

"Snipper!" exclaimed the other. He sounded shocked. It was clear he knew the name and equally clear that Snipper's sudden appearance was most unwelcome. "You won't find your friend here."

"So where *will* I find her?"

"You've already been told - she was taken by the Verdissians."

"For pity's sake!" pleaded Snipper. "Why can't someone just tell me the truth? If it's a ransom you want, say so!"

"How did you find us?" asked the other hedgehog, ignoring Snipper's outburst.

"I tailed you, " said Snipper. He took a deep breath to recover his composure. "From your meeting with Count de Poynte. The door was unlocked."

The other hedgehog stared at Snipper for a moment, his whiskers twitching ever so slightly. Snipper thought he seemed nervous. Certainly de Poynte was unlikely to be impressed by their security arrangements.

"Look, I'm sorry," said Snipper, thinking he should get out while he still could. "I'd no right to barge in here. I'll go now." He made a move towards the door, but the other hedgehog barred his exit.

"Wait," commanded the other. He got out his phone and made a call. When it was answered, he said something - or sang something - in a language which sounded like no other on Earth. Then he offered the phone to Snipper. "It's Commander Woad – the hedgehog you know as Count de Poynte," he explained. "He wants to speak to you."

"Hello?" said Snipper, taking the phone.

"You're a very persistent hedgehog," said Woad.

"I just want to find my friend."

"Of course. But how much? How far would you really be prepared to go for her?"

"I'd go to the ends of the world for Despina," said Snipper anxiously, wondering where this was leading.

"Oh, but you'll have to go considerably further than that."

Hearing the same old story, Snipper had to resist the temptation to ring off. "You're going to burgle the Astellaritz space factory, aren't you?" he said. "Why? What's it got to do with Despina's abduction?"

"It has nothing to do with her abduction," said Woad with a sigh of impatience. "*We* have nothing to do with her abduction. But listen. We may be able to help you find her. We have someone on the inside. And, if you're willing to come with us, I'm willing to lay on a rescue mission."

"When?" asked Snipper. He did not bother to ask where. He knew he would be given the same old answer – Verdis.

"On Thursday. That's the earliest we can be ready."

"All right," agreed Snipper. "I'll come back then." Although he still did not believe the story about Verdis and hedgehogs from outer space, he felt unable to refuse the offer. In the meantime, he would have three days in which to continue his own investigation.

"Oh, I'm afraid you won't be going anywhere in the meantime," said Woad. "You know too much. I won't run the risk of you going to the police. Now pass me back to my colleague."

Though Snipper had no intention of staying put for the next three days, he made no attempt to reason with Woad. Passing the phone back in silence, he then listened in fascination while there was a brief but very tuneful conversation. Then he was taken down to the kitchen, where the tubby hedgehog and their driver were just pouring themselves a hot drink. They were naturally startled to see him. But, after a brief explanation from their colleague, they relaxed and everyone was finally introduced. The tall and tubby hedgehogs announced themselves as Lieutenants Lappis and Lazzuli of the Cerulean Space Force. The driver gave her name as Space Cadet Cyanne.

"So you mean..." said Snipper, hesitantly. Somehow he could hardly bring himself to say it out loud – it sounded so foolish. "You're telling me you're... that you, as well as Count de Poynte – or Commander Woad or whatever he's called, are from outer space."

"We are," said Lieutenant Lappis in the most matter-of-fact way possible. "Now, enough questions - "

"If he's staying," said Lieutenant Lazzuli, "he can make himself useful. There's a pile of washing up over there which needs doing."

For a moment Snipper wondered whether he had heard right. Over the course of his career as a secret agent, he had been threatened, imprisoned and beaten up. Once he had even been dumped in a wilderness and left to die. But no one had ever told him to do their washing up before. He reckoned that, on the whole, they were letting him off rather lightly, given he had just been caught going through their things.

"All right," he said. "Just let me text my friends first or they'll worry. When shall I tell them I'll be back?"

"You can text them later," said Lappis. "After you've finished washing up."

Snipper rather doubted they intended to let him communicate with his friends at all, even after he had done their chores for them. He would have to find a moment when they were not looking. In the meantime, he rolled up his sleeves and got going on the dishes. It was hard work, as the stuff had clearly been sitting around for a while and there was an awful lot of it. Eventually, however, he finished and was rewarded with a cup of tea, which he took gratefully. They even allowed him to sit at the kitchen table with them. And for a while he just sat there, silently sipping his tea, watching this mysterious band of hedgehogs as they examined a piece of machinery. He got the impression it was faulty though he had no idea what it was. In fact, they seemed so intent on their examination and so singularly uninterested in him that it seemed like a good moment to try texting Pawline.

Snipper reached into his pocket for his phone; but, as he did so, he was suddenly conscious of a curious numbness in his paws. He found himself fumbling so badly that he was unable to operate the thing at all. If only the phone were not so far away it might be a little easier. And if only he were not so very tired... so very, very tired... Gradually, a vague realization crept into Snipper's fuzzy head that his tea had been drugged. He prodded a claw into his leg in an effort to resist, but his leg seemed to have lost all feeling. As he sat there, unable to move, he tried hard to think. Why had they...? Who...? But the thoughts were confused, formless - random even. As he slumped forwards, he heard someone get up. His phone was taken from him and his pockets were searched. The ID cards and holographic projector were swiftly removed. Snipper wondered whether it was really so important to stay awake. If only he could sleep - even just for a few seconds, he would feel so much better...

He slept. Once or twice, he started to surface. But then there would be a sharp, pricking sensation in his arm, and he would feel himself falling into a deep and irresistible slumber. The first time it happened, he was vaguely aware of faces - an array of hedgehogs bending over him, singing tunefully to one another. The second time, he found himself being carried along a path. It seemed to be night, but he could just make out the glint of a lake ahead and the silhouette of a seaplane. Then there were more voices and that pricking sensation... Then sleep.

Chapter Four

Later - hours, days or perhaps even months later, for all he knew - Snipper began to surface once more. His first sensation as he began to come round was one of intense, clawing hunger. Then gradually he became aware of his surroundings - the throbbing of an engine, heat, airlessness and a faint smell of diesel. As he opened his eyes, he fully expected to feel the needle in his arm again; but this time nothing happened. Instead, little by little, he shed the layers of sleep which had enveloped him.

Yet even as he began to feel fully awake he thought he must surely be dreaming. Looking around, he found himself in a small aeroplane with four hedgehogs wearing a uniform of some sort. Their faces were strangely familiar. In fact, they were identical to Count de Poynte and his cronies in every respect except one.

"You're blue," said Snipper bluntly.

"Of course," said de Poynte. "I've already explained this to you. I'm afraid your limited experience of the universe and, let us say, rather basic Earthling science has stopped you from accepting a simple fact."

Snipper stared at de Poynte and his crew. If there really was a chemical solution to change a hedgehog's colour, was it not more probable that these were brown hedgehogs pretending to be blue rather

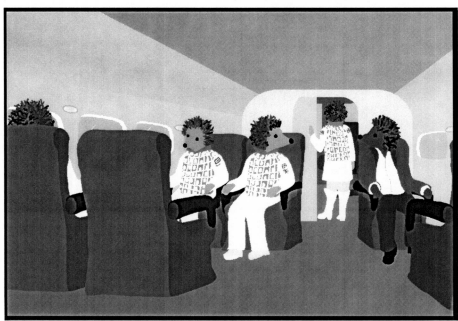

than the other way around? But why would they do that? He no longer knew what to think. It all seemed too elaborate to be a charade. Whatever the case, the most pressing thing now was to find out where they were taking him. He looked out of the window, but all he could see was a vast expanse of water: they might be anywhere.

"Where are we going?"

"To Verdis – to get Despina, as we agreed."

"But this is an ordinary seaplane..."

"We'll be transferring to the spaceplane shortly."

"I see," said Snipper, hesitantly. Resist as he might, he found he was actually beginning to believe Count de Poynte – or Commander Woad, as he felt he should now start calling him. The thought made him feel queasy. And feeling queasy reminded him that he had just come out of a drug-induced stupor. Perhaps the drug had done something to his mind. Perhaps he was hallucinating. "Why did you drug me?" he demanded.

"I'm afraid we had no choice," said Woad. "My colleagues were far too busy to keep an eye on you. And they said you seemed troublesome. If you'd slipped away and led the police to us, that would at best have delayed our departure. At worst, well..."

"Busy burgling the Astellaritz space factory, you mean," said Snipper pointedly.

"I'm sorry if you disapprove," said Woad - though Snipper thought he did not sound sorry at all. "We needed spare parts."

Snipper shrugged his shoulders and fell silent. A spot of burglary seemed the least of his concerns right now. He glanced out of the window. There was still no sign of a launch pad - or even of land. Neither could he get any signal on his phone. But there were several messages welcoming him to various countries, indicating a south-westerly course from Hedgermany; the last had been sent five hours ago. Snipper did a quick calculation. Based on their current speed and assuming a straight course, they must be virtually on the equator by now. Suddenly he remembered the unmarked dot on the Ceruleans' holographic globe. Then he remembered Pawline back in Hedgermany, who would be three thousand miles away by now and probably frantic with worry. Scrolling down through his Inbox, he found four messages from her.

Snipper, read the first, *your message has upset me more than I can say. Despina's our friend. I'm desperately worried about her and I thought you were too. So how can you make up such stories? Are you unwell? Must I worry about you as well as Despina? Tell me where you are. We'll come and collect you.*

Snipper frowned. What message was she talking about?

"Are you worrying about your friends?" asked Woad, when he saw Snipper staring at his mobile. "There's no need. I sent Pawline a message from your phone before we left Hedgermany."

"*You* did!" exclaimed Snipper. "How do you know about Pawline? I never mentioned her to you."

"Despina did."

"I see," said Snipper. "So what exactly did you...?" He stopped mid-sentence and checked his phone instead.

I've found out where Despina is, read the message. *As soon as you get this, go to Milchnicht railway station. Open locker 11 (combination 20-07-69). You'll find a packet containing some spines belonging to Count de Poynte. Get Schnüffel to analyse the DNA and he'll tell you that de Poynte is not from Earth. I can tell you more. De Poynte is from a planet called Cerulea. He witnessed Despina's abduction and recognized the hedgehogs who took her - Verdissians, from a neighbouring planet.*

I've now gone with de Poynte to rescue Despina and I'll be out of contact for a while. I need you to report all this to the International Space Agency. Tell them the Verdissians have discovered our planet and will be back. They're space pirates who take anything and anyone they can lay their paws on. De Poynte believes they took Despina as a sample Earthling to exhibit back home. Once they've generated enough interest, they'll be back for more - to sell as slaves on Verdis. Tell the agency we cannot defend ourselves against the Verdissians. We must put ourselves under Cerulean protection. We must be ready to accept any offer of help we get.

"You're saying they took Despina to be their slave!" exclaimed Snipper, appalled by what he read. "How do you know this?"

"It's the only possible explanation," said Woad. "The Verdissians are pirates. They've already stripped other planets of all their natural resources - turning into deserts places which might have supported life one day. Now they know about your planet, whose resources are far richer than those of any other they've ever visited. And clearly it isn't only minerals and crops they're interested in. Earthlings are an easy source of cheap labour. How could they resist?"

"But why are *you* doing all this?" asked Snipper. "Helping me - us?"

44

"Well, to be frank, that wasn't my original intention. As I mentioned before, our policy is not to interfere in Earthling affairs. But you were very persistent, and I began to feel a little guilty. For I'm afraid we Ceruleans must take some of the blame for what's happened. When we discovered Earth - six months ago by your reckoning, we were determined to keep our discovery secret. We knew that, if the Verdissians found out about it, they'd show no mercy. But, for all the care we took, they *have* found out; and they must have done so through us - the universe is too vast for this to be a coincidence."

"What about the Cerulean authorities? What do *they* think of all this?"

"I haven't yet reported the incident to the Cerulean High Command. That won't be possible until we're back in our own solar system - which unfortunately we share with the Verdissians."

Snipper frowned. Somewhere at the back of his mind he must have known that Cerulea and Verdis lay in another solar system. But until now he had paid little attention to Woad's ramblings about outer space. It was only as he began to believe him that the thought struck: if Cerulea and Verdis lay in the very next solar system, that was still 4.2 light years away – in other words, twenty-five trillion miles. Even if it were possible to travel at the speed of light, it would still take them more than four years to get there.

"Surely if the Verdissians don't know we're on their tail," said Snipper, a little anxiously, "we must stand a good chance of overtaking them. Wouldn't it be better to intercept their spaceship rather than follow them all the way back to Verdis?"

"Intergalactic space travel is much faster than you think. We'll be there in no time at all. Just a matter of a few Earth days... or months, depending on how you look at it."

Snipper felt as though his mind were about to explode. Woad was now talking about *intergalactic* space travel. That meant travelling not just to another solar system but to a different galaxy altogether. The closest galaxy to Earth's own lay 2.5 million light years away. Snipper tried to convert the light years into miles in his head but gave up. It had to be something in the order of billions of trillions of miles.

"Intergalactic travel!" exclaimed Snipper. "How can that even be possible? And how would we find Despina once we got there? It would be like looking for a needle in a haystack. We stand a far better chance of finding her while she's still on the spaceship."

"You forget the Verdissians have a significant head start on us," responded Woad. "We can't catch up. But your doubts about us covering the distance are illogical. We got here. Going back will be no different. And you can rest assured that, when we do arrive, we will locate Despina. We have a hedgehog on the inside who can help us, so it should all be pretty straightforward. Besides, the Verdissians won't be expecting us."

"Shall we go in under cover of darkness?"

"Only if they've taken her to the Dark Side."

"What's the Dark Side?" asked Snipper. Though he had no idea what it was, he did not much like the sound of it.

"Verdis rotates very slowly," explained Woad. "One Verdissian day lasts 225 Earth days - longer than a Verdissian year, which is only 180 Earth days. So the Verdissians don't experience night and day as Earthlings do - or, indeed, as we do on Cerulea. Instead, they divide their planet in two and set up home accordingly. Naturally, most prefer to live on the Light Side, but a few choose the Dark Side - you'll find a number of observatories, research stations and high security prisons located there."

"What happens when the Light Side goes dark and vice versa?"

"They're nomadic – they move."

"I see. So, if Despina's on the Light Side, how will you go in undetected?"

"We'll be disguised as Verdissians. We have a special chemical solution - "

"Which turns you green?"

"Just so."

"And what do you think will happen when the Verdissians realize Despina's gone?"

"They'll guess it was us. After all, who else? Just as it was obvious to us," added Woad grimly, "that our two spacecraft which recently went missing on the very same day must have been captured by the Verdissians."

"Couldn't that have just been an accident?" asked Snipper, who did not like to jump to conclusions.

"What? Both of them? Both carrying a valuable cargo and then disappearing without trace? I don't think so. The Verdissians attacked and looted those spacecraft - and then destroyed them so there'd be no evidence... and no witnesses."

Snipper began to see there was more to Woad's offer of help than just making amends. He clearly detested the Verdissians. Despina's abduction might have merely furnished him with the excuse he had been waiting for to strike a blow at the enemy. Yet Snipper could hardly complain. Without the Ceruleans' help, he had no hope of finding Despina and Earth would be unable to stop the Verdissians from returning. Snipper hoped Pawline had taken Woad's prodding and reported the situation to the International Space Agency. Of course, that would be only the first step. The many nations of Earth would then have to come together and agree a course of action; they would also have to ask for Cerulean help. But, without Pawline's co-operation, no one would even know about the lurking Verdissian threat. Everything rested in her paws.

Snipper returned to his inbox and read the three unopened messages from Pawline. In the second and third, she simply urged Snipper to get in contact with her. In the fourth, she assured him she had picked up the packet containing Woad's spines and passed it to Schnüffel for testing. Snipper wondered if she had or was just humouring him. But there was no way of finding out now, for he had long since lost his phone signal.

"Snipper, you'd better tighten your seat belt. We'll be landing soon."

It was Space Cadet Cyanne speaking – the driver of the black saloon car back in Hedgermany. As she sat down opposite him, she smiled. It was a warm, sympathetic smile which made Snipper reflect. Though Woad was doing him a huge favour, there was something cold about him - something oddly unsympathetic about his manner.

Snipper was pondering over this question, when he felt the plane go into a steep descent. Looking out of the window, he saw two huge floating platforms come into view. On the first there were two satellite dishes and what looked like an observatory. On the second there was a spaceplane.

Chapter Five

Snipper stared in amazement. Any lingering doubts were finally dispelled. These strange blue hedgehogs really were who they claimed to be - aliens from outer space. They had been telling the truth all along. Despina's abduction now struck him with fresh horror, as he finally understood that she really had been taken by space pirates.

The depth of his ignorance - along with his utter helplessness - was suddenly laid bare. Though he was well educated in Earthling terms, it now turned out the Earth itself was a mere speck in a vast and ancient universe, of which he knew almost nothing. But, if Snipper felt overwhelmed, how must Despina be feeling? At least he had the Ceruleans on his side. She, on the other hand, had been kidnapped by Verdissians who would look down upon her as an inferior being. Frightened, friendless and alone, she could feel no hope of ever returning to Earth.

A sudden jolt forwards as the seaplane touched the water brought Snipper back to the here and now. Looking out, he saw spray fly up around the plane's floats as they skidded over the waves, before making full contact with the sea. Then the engine fell silent and gradually the plane decelerated. When they had finally come to a halt, a dinghy came to pick them up. As he stepped outside, Snipper felt a wave of pleasure at being out in the fresh air again, after so many hours cooped up. Sniffing the salty sea air, feeling the sun's warmth and the ruffle of the sea breeze through his spines, he felt reinvigorated. His thoughts turned briefly to food: he had not eaten for three days and was very hungry. But an empty stomach was perhaps a good thing if he was about to be blasted into space. Indeed, the very thought of his imminent launch made him feel queasy. The prospect of the lift-off - for which he had received no instruction - was itself bad enough. But was he really prepared to be sent into outer space with a bunch of hedgehogs he had met only three days ago? When he had agreed to go with them, he had not believed they were really going into space. And what did he know about any of them? But what alternative did he have? He had virtually been kidnapped himself. And leaving Despina to her fate was not an option.

Arriving beneath the launch platform, their dinghy was tossed around in a confusion of waves, as the sea crashed against the platform legs. It was not a place to linger. Lappis, Lazzuli and Woad hurried into the lift. Waiting his turn with Cyanne, Snipper watched the seaplane taxi round to the far side of the platform and unload its cargo. First off were a couple of crates containing the small blue cylinders from the boathouse on Igelininsel. These were followed by a series of boxes, suitcases and other items. To his surprise, Snipper noticed his own suitcase among them. The Ceruleans must have fetched it from his hotel. He wondered idly whether they had also paid his bill...

But by now the lift was back, and it was Snipper's turn to go up with Cyanne. A minute later, they had been whisked up onto the platform; the ocean was left far behind. Stepping out, Snipper found himself just feet away from the Cerulean spaceplane, which towered above him. It looked an impossibly simple machine. Apparently made from a single sheet of metal, it also lacked any external fuel tanks. Snipper wondered how on earth it could be carrying enough fuel to propel itself into space - let alone halfway across the universe. As for the tiny wings near its base, they seemed far too small to be of any use at all.

With a mental shrug of his shoulders, Snipper followed the others into a building at the far end of the platform, where they were given their space suits, ventilators and anti-sickness pills. Snipper was helped into his suit by Cyanne, who arranged and fastened its many flaps and seals to ensure it was airtight. Then, when they were all suited up and ready to go, they made their way over to the spaceplane.

The entrance was a circular hatch high up towards the tip, accessed by another lift. As they waited for their turn in the lift, Snipper and Cyanne were joined by Flight Lieutenant Azziur and Pilot Officer Sapphire, who had been flying the seaplane and would now be flying the spaceplane. The two pilots greeted Snipper with a laid-back assurance which reminded him strongly of airline pilots. It made him wonder how many times they had flown back and forth in this spaceplane before.

On the short walkway at the top, Snipper paused to take one last look around him. He was thousands of miles from home, in the middle of a vast and inhospitable ocean. Yet right now, as he considered what lay ahead, even this felt like home. Wistfully, he tracked a lone cloud drifting gracefully across the sky. He watched the glint of sunlight upon the ocean waves and breathed the salty air deep into his lungs. Then he turned round and followed the others inside.

Snipper entered the flight deck at 90° - stepping onto what was actually its back wall. Though broadly similar to the cockpit of an aeroplane, there were a great many more screens and buttons. Running down the centre of the deck were three rows of seats, accessed by ladders. Cyanne helped Snipper up into his and then strapped herself in beside him. Snipper now watched as the Ceruleans prepared for lift-off, checking the systems to ensure everything was working. Just as

they finished, the last two crew members arrived - who were also, according to Cyanne, the last two members of the Ceruleans' eight-strong landing party.

The hatch was now closed and the final checks were carried out. For a moment, everything went quiet. Then Snipper felt the rocket vibrate. There was a low rumble, which grew steadily louder, and then the countdown to lift-off - unmistakable in any language.

At first it was difficult to tell they had left the ground. But then Snipper felt his back being pressed into the seat. Steadily the pressure built until eventually it felt as though a giant paw were pressing down against his chest. Just as it was beginning to verge on the unbearable, the pressure first eased and then disappeared altogether. Someone pointed at a small toy, tied to the dashboard with a piece of string. The string was slack and the toy was drifting slowly upwards: Snipper was in space.

It had taken just eight minutes. Strapped to his seat, he had no clear sensation of weightlessness. But he felt puffy and congested, as though he had a cold coming on. Above all, he felt dazed. By rights, he should have been travelling to the United Stakes next week to watch Pawline's launch into space - the culmination of years of hard training. Instead, here was he, going into space with no training at all. He would not only miss her big day but had even beaten her to it. And, while she would be orbiting the Earth, he was bound for a distant galaxy, the passenger of an alien crew...

But Pawline could be confident of her return to Earth. She knew exactly what she was getting into. She was an active and important member of her mission and, training on mock-ups, already knew the international space station like the back of her paw. She knew her daily timetable for the next six months. She understood the science. And, above all, she knew and trusted her colleagues. Snipper, on the other hand, was just a passenger and had very little idea of what he was getting himself into. He could not even be sure he would ever come back. If only he could have found out a little more before setting off. But now was no time to be distracting the crew with questions. So he kept these for later and instead watched them quietly.

Much of the time, the crew were simply monitoring their screens. During these moments, Snipper gazed out of the window at the stars. But occasionally there would be a flurry of activity, as they pushed a few buttons and sang tunefully to each other.

It was only when the Moon came into view that Snipper realized quite how far they had come – 230,000 miles in little more than an hour (the last Earthlings to come this way had taken three days). The craters, valleys and mountains which made up the familiar face of the Moon could now be clearly distinguished. But, as they swung round to the far side, Snipper's attention was grabbed by something else. A large asteroid seemed to be orbiting the Moon. Had the Earth's satellite now acquired a satellite of its own? His question was answered a moment later as he saw the object morph from an asteroid into an enormous and extraordinary-looking spaceship. For a second, he thought they must have caught up with the Verdissians after all. Then he noticed the spaceplane docked onto it, which was identical to their own. His hopes and fears subsided together.

The Cerulean spaceship was many times larger than their rocket and unlike it in every way. Around its core was a huge rotating wheel. The ship was also equipped with solar panels and four giant sails. The sails puzzled Snipper at first. But then he remembered the invisible but ferocious force of the solar wind, which radiated from the sun and from which Earth was protected by its magnetic field.

Approaching the spaceship, they slowed down to a snail's pace - inching forwards until they were directly over the docking port. For a few minutes they simply hovered, making minute adjustments to their position. Then there was a clunk. They had made contact.

The crew now unstrapped themselves and floated off towards the door. Following their example, Snipper freed himself but then found he was starting to drift upwards. He stretched out his paw to prevent himself from bumping into the ceiling but the next moment was bouncing back down towards the floor. He would need to be gentler. Cyanne turned round and offered him her paw. Taking it gratefully, he glided behind her, over towards the exit and out into the docking station, where several members of the spaceship's crew had lined up to greet their colleagues. One of them was listening intently to Woad and every now and again glanced at Snipper. The badge on his uniform was fancier than the others' and he seemed to be questioning Woad with an air of authority. Snipper remembered the Cerulean authorities' policy of non-interference in the affairs of Earth. He wondered how they would feel about his presence on their ship, but he could detect neither disapproval nor even surprise. And, when Woad had finished speaking, the other hedgehog beckoned Snipper forward.

"Welcome on board the *ISV Resurgence*," said the hedgehog, speaking in Snipper's native tongue. "Though I don't suppose you know what an ISV is. Well, it's an interstellar space vehicle. And I'm Captain Cobalt, the commander of this ship."

"How d'you do?" responded Snipper. "My name's Snipper. I'm er... I'm from Earth," he added rather pointlessly.

"Yes, I know who you are. Commander Woad has given me a full report. Your presence here is, of course, a direct contravention of Cerulean policy. As soon as we're back in our own solar system, the matter of Despina's rescue and your own involvement with us will be referred to the High Command. In the meantime, please consider yourself our guest. Space Cadet Cyanne will show you to your quarters."

On hearing this indirect order, Cyanne promptly whisked Snipper away. They continued for a while down the same corridor, gliding along until the floor suddenly disappeared from beneath them. For a moment they seemed to be floating above a long vertical shaft. Snipper peered down gingerly – though he knew perfectly well that in space there was no up or down - everything was relative to one's own position.

Cyanne stretched out her paw and pushed off against the ceiling - or what passed for a ceiling at the present moment. Copying her, Snipper tipped forwards so that the ceiling became the wall behind him and the vertical shaft below him was now just an ordinary corridor in front of him. On reaching the end of this corridor, they entered a small cubicle. Inside were a couple of chairs, fixed to the wall at right angles and equipped with seat belts. With a gentle push of the feet, Cyanne and Snipper floated up towards the two chairs and, grabbing hold of them, pulled themselves down onto the seats and strapped themselves in. Then Cyanne sang some sort of instruction to an invisible computer and the cubicle began to move, gradually building up speed. Snipper got the distinct impression of descending in a lift. He wondered if it was just because they were travelling feet first. A few seconds later, the cubicle came to a halt and Cyanne got out of her seat. Snipper noticed she was standing firmly rooted to the floor. A moment later, so was he.

"Fascinating!" murmured Snipper, half speaking to himself. "So that giant rotating wheel..."

"That's right," said Cyanne. "It creates an outward force, mimicking the effect of gravity. You see, these are our living quarters and we aim to live here as normally as possible. Of course, it's also important to avoid the harmful effects of long-term weightlessness."

Leaving the cubicle through another door, they now walked down a corridor dotted with display cases full of medals and other trophies.

The walls were lined with portraits of distinguished-looking blue hedgehogs in uniform. Snipper's own room was large and very comfortably furnished. A glass door led out onto a small, private conservatory full of flowers and shrubs. For a moment he was surprised by the lack of external windows; then he remembered they were inside a giant wheel rotating at enormous speed. The view would probably have made him dizzy. Right now, having gone without food for so long, he felt light-headed just thinking about it. He sank onto the sofa. Looking around, he noticed his suitcase, which had been left next to the bed. He gazed at it fondly. It looked terribly out of place.

"I expect you'd like to get some rest now," said Cyanne.

"Actually, I could really do with something to eat," said Snipper. "After all, I've had nothing for three days."

"I'll get the kitchen to send you something. Is there anything else you need?"

"Well, I've got quite a few questions I'd like to ask you."

"All right," said Cyanne. She pressed a button on her uniform, sang a brief snatch of melody and then pressed the button again. "What do you want to know?"

"Well, first of all, exactly how long is this voyage going to be? I mean, even if your galaxy is right next door to ours, that's still billions of trillions of miles away. And, given we can't travel faster than the speed of light, it's surely going to take us quite a few lifetimes to reach Verdis... I mean, it *isn't* possible to travel faster than the speed of light, is it?" added Snipper hesitantly. "Or have I got that wrong as well?"

"It isn't necessary," said Cyanne. "Have you heard of wormholes?"

"Yes... though I'm not entirely sure what they are."

"Well, Snipper," said Cyanne rather deliberately, as though she were about to explain something to a young and none too bright hoglet, "all around us, there are tiny, microscopic holes in the fabric of space-time. Sometimes these holes are so deep they link up with other holes, creating shortcuts. These shortcuts are what you Earthlings call wormholes, and they can lead anywhere. Some only lead to another part of the same solar system - in fact, you could emerge just a few feet away from where you started. But others will take you to the farthest flung corners of the universe."

"And how long does it take to travel through one of these wormholes?"

"That really depends upon your point of view. You see, time is relative and can be experienced differently by different hedgehogs. From the point of view of anyone *outside* the wormhole, the journey takes no time at all. In fact, if it were possible to be at both ends of a wormhole at once, observing a spaceship enter and exit, this would appear as one smooth continuous movement. The spaceship wouldn't disappear - not even for a second. So, seen from that point of view, the journey is instant - you can travel from one end of the universe to another in literally no time at all."

"And if you're *inside* the spaceship that's travelling through the wormhole?" prompted Snipper.

"That varies from wormhole to wormhole. No two are completely alike, but it can take up to three or four months."

"Months!" exclaimed Snipper. The thought of Despina alone on a Verdissian spaceship for so long filled him with horror. "And when exactly will we reach our wormhole?"

"That's difficult to say," responded Cyanne with an amused smile. "You can never use the same wormhole twice. In their natural form, they're tiny and collapse within seconds. When you do find one, you have to stabilize it and then expand it so it's safe enough and big enough to enter. Only then can you send through a probe to see what's at the other end - to see whether the shortcut will take you where you want to go. So just finding a suitable wormhole can take several hours. But it's the same for the Verdissians. We won't be so very far behind them and, after all, we know where they're headed." Cyanne smiled at Snipper and placed a paw on his arm. "Don't worry, Snipper. You will see your friend again."

The arrival of Snipper's food put a sudden end to this conversation. Cyanne left him with a promise to return later and show him round the spaceship. Sitting down to his meal, Snipper now mulled over her attempt to reassure him. Her concern had touched him, and he suddenly realized it was the first indication of empathy he had received from any of the Ceruleans. But a growl from his stomach brought his thoughts back to food. Examining the strange little collection of Cerulean food dishes on his tray, he wondered whether it would be enough. In the event, the meal proved surprisingly satisfying, though it was nowhere near as tasty as the meals he was used to on Earth. He seemed to remember Schnüffel praising the food on the international space station. But perhaps it was all relative - like time.

Following the meal, Snipper showered and put on a fresh set of clothes. Then he unpacked his battered old suitcase and arranged his few familiar possessions around the room: paints and paper, camera, a pack of cards, a guidebook to Milchnicht and a book on the construction of the international space station. Last but not least, he opened out the programme from Despina's concert and set it on his bedside table. On the front cover was a photograph of Despina.

Surrounded by her fellow musicians, she gazed happily at the photographer, blissfully unaware of what awaited her.

The tour of the spaceship started on the bridge. This was back in the weightless zone, but Captain Cobalt and his crew were all strapped into their seats, while Cyanne and Snipper floated unobtrusively by the door. Snipper's attention was drawn irresistibly to the huge window above them and the stars beyond, until a sudden flurry of activity distracted him. Clearly something had happened, for Cobalt and his crew suddenly burst into song.

"What's happened?" whispered Snipper.

"They've found a wormhole."

"They have!" exclaimed Snipper excitedly. "Will it do?"

"We don't know yet. They've just stabilized it but they still have to expand it and send in a probe. It'll be a little while yet before they can tell where it goes. Chances are it won't do, but that's OK. There are plenty more out there and they can analyse more than one at a time. Come on, I'll show you the observation deck. I think you'll like it."

Snipper liked the observation deck very much. A simple glass sphere, it was attached to the main body of the spaceship by a long tubular corridor. It therefore stood well away from the rest of the ship, giving an almost 360° view of space. Floating around the glass sphere, Snipper felt as though he were out among the stars, drifting free in space. The delight of weightlessness was stronger than ever. Then, doing a somersault, Snipper suddenly caught sight of Earth. Far, far away now, his planet appeared no bigger than his paw. Yet surely there could be nothing more beautiful than this. A bright blue shining globe, floating in a sea of darkness - so precious and yet so fragile. To think that everything he knew and everyone he loved was contained within it - everyone, except for Despina.

For the final stop on Cyanne's tour of the spaceship, they returned to the weighted zone. With their feet now firmly back on the ground, the two hedgehogs made their way to the communal living area. Here off-duty members of the crew lounged on sofas - chatting, playing games and reading. At first glance, it looked as though they were playing board games and reading old-fashioned paper books. But a second glance revealed these to be holographic projections. Cyanne took Snipper over to a dispensing machine and sang to it. Out popped a small black cylinder just like the one on Igelininsel.

"There you are. Some reading material for the voyage."

Snipper took it and pressed the button on its side. A solid 3D image of a book appeared. He touched it with his paw; it felt solid and real.

"Now just say what you want to read about," said Cyanne.

Snipper looked at her quizzically. Surely she was not expecting him to speak Cerulean.

"Go on, speak!" she urged. "It's programmed to respond to several Earthling languages."

"Astronomy!" said Snipper. The words *Encyclopaedia of the Universe* suddenly appeared on the hitherto blank cover.

"Very impressive," he said, "but how do I browse?"

"I'm afraid that's it on astronomy. You'd have been given options if any other books had been translated."

Snipper was surprised. He had rather assumed that, with all their technology, every Cerulean book could have been translated at the touch of a button. He was about to say so, when an announcement over the loudspeaker prevented him. Everyone in the room suddenly stopped what they were doing to listen. And, when the message had finished, they all left.

"What is it?" he asked. "What's happened?"

"We're about to enter the wormhole," said Cyanne, with evident excitement. "Let's go and watch from the observation deck."

They reached the observation deck just in time. The wormhole

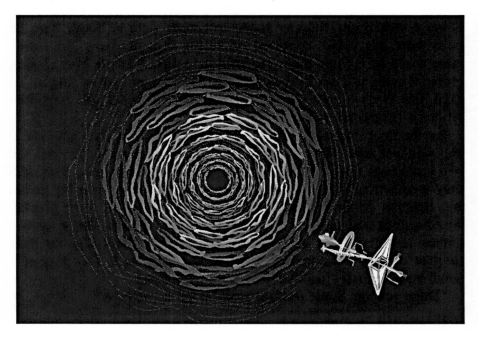

which so recently had been microscopically small was now vast. Though invisible itself, its presence was marked by a distortion – as though the stars were wrapped around a huge transparent sphere. But, as the spaceship passed over the wormhole horizon, the stars around them grew steadily dimmer until finally they disappeared, leaving only an inky blackness. A moment later there was a blinding flash of light. The spaceship began to shake violently; but, almost as soon as it had started, it stopped. They were now right inside the wormhole, and it was a beautiful sight: the spaceship was enveloped by swirling ribbons of light and dust. Snipper would have been content to stay watching this extraordinary show, but a bell rang, summoning them away.

"They're announcing the start of Hibernival," explained Cyanne as she led Snipper back to the living quarters. "I hope you're still hungry!"

"What's Hibernival?" asked Snipper.

"It's the great week-long feast to build up our energy stores before we go into hibernation... Oh, I forgot - you Earthlings don't hibernate."

Snipper found Cyanne's tone a little patronising. Though few in number, there *were* Earthlings who knew how to hibernate - and he was one of them. He had learnt it as part of his Secret Service training. In fact, back in the mists of time, all Earthlings had hibernated to get through the winter. But these days that was no longer necessary and few had even heard of it. Of course, Snipper could have explained this to Cyanne but he chose to keep it to himself. As a secret agent, his first instinct was always to keep his cards close to his chest.

"No, I don't suppose we do hibernate," said Snipper, somewhat disingenuously. "What exactly does it involve?"

"We shut down," explained Cyanne. "We reduce our breathing, our heartbeat - everything, by about ninety per cent. It reduces the wear and tear on our bodies and puts a break on the ageing process. So, when we go home, we don't find we've aged several months more than everyone else. You see, going back and forth through wormholes could add up to a difference of years."

"Yes, I can imagine that would be a problem," said Snipper. "So do you all hibernate? Or will there be a skeleton crew operating the ship?"

"I'm afraid it'll just be you," said Cyanne. "We put the ship on autopilot. Will you mind?"

"Not too much," said Snipper breezily. "I've never been a particularly social animal." Snipper was a little surprised the Ceruleans would trust him enough to give him the run of their ship while they hibernated. Perhaps they felt they had nothing to fear from a simple Earthling. Whatever the case, the chance to explore the place without an official guide - even a friendly one like Cyanne - had to be welcomed. "So what gets you out of hibernation?" he asked. "Is there some sort of communal alarm clock?"

"The ship's programmed to turn the heating up as we approach the end of the wormhole. You see, it has to be pretty chilly for us to hibernate. It can't be more than 2° centigrade. And it's the returning warmth that wakes us."

"I see. So shall I be cold as well as lonely?" asked Snipper with a wry smile.

"No, we'll be in a different part of the spaceship - on the hibernation deck. You'll be in the living quarters. We can leave the heating on there and turn it down everywhere else."

The Hibernival feast was held on the vast dining deck. When Snipper and Cyanne arrived, the room was filling up fast. Six long trestle tables occupied most of the room and, by the time everyone was seated, Snipper guessed there must be about three hundred hedgehogs present. But they would not be going hungry. Unlike his own relatively modest meal, the food provided now was plentiful. To the casual observer it might even have smacked of gluttony. But Snipper knew that stoking up for a lengthy hibernation was a serious business, and they would need to eat a great deal.

Cyanne and Snipper found space on a bench alongside Azziur and Sapphire. The two pilots nodded silently to them and then resumed their eating. Snipper noticed there was remarkably little chatter generally. But this gradually changed as the eaters began to have their fill.

"You'll have to do better than that," said Sapphire, turning to Snipper, who had eaten very modestly. "Aren't you feeling well?"

"Snipper won't be hibernating," explained Cyanne. "He doesn't know how."

"Why not?" asked Sapphire. She seemed amused.

"No Earthlings do," explained Azziur. "They don't have any reason to - after all, they haven't mastered space travel yet."

Snipper was about to object that Earthlings had travelled to the Moon and sent space probes out of their solar system; then he thought better of it. These would be primitive achievements in the eyes of the Ceruleans, who could apparently travel anywhere in the universe.

"So what are you going to do with yourself for the next few months?" asked Azziur.

"If you're at a loose end," said Sapphire, before Snipper had time to respond, "my medal collection could really do with a polish - "

"I suspect," interrupted Azziur, "Snipper's got more interesting things to do with his time than polish your medals."

"Well yes, I'm afraid I have," said Snipper, though he had no intention of telling them what his real plans were. "For one thing, I've got my watercolours with me. I so seldom have the time to paint back on Earth that I'll be glad to have the opportunity here."

Snipper's first week in space went more slowly than he had expected. A great deal of his time was spent on the dining deck, either eating or watching the crew eat - mostly the latter. There was seldom much conversation. Any questions about Cerulea and Verdis would be met with answers so brief and to the point as to discourage much further discussion. Eventually, however, he did manage to piece together a sketchy picture of the two planets. Verdis and Cerulea circled a single sun, the only inhabited planets in their solar system. Verdis was the inner and the warmer of the two. Cerulea was not only further from its sun, but its extreme elliptical orbit was currently taking it still further away. Much of the planet was now covered in ice. But the Ceruleans had apparently risen to the challenge of their tough environment, demonstrating an adaptability and self-reliance which were the envy of the Verdissians.

As for Cerulean and Verdissian space travel, this had a long history, but for most of it they had been confined to their own solar system. It was just twenty Earth years ago that the Ceruleans had finally learnt how to stabilize and expand wormholes. Since then they had travelled unimaginable distances - seeking answers to life, the universe and everything. They had visited countless planets. Yet all of them were devoid of life, until six months ago, when they discovered Earth.

It had seemed like a miracle, when they stumbled upon this beautiful blue planet with everything - air, water, a favourable climate, a magnetic shield and even life itself. The Ceruleans' first instinct was to visit Earth openly, without disguise - to make themselves known to the inhabitants. But, when they learnt of the primitive state of Earthling science and technology, they changed their minds. They feared the appearance of a more advanced species would disrupt the natural evolution of Earthling knowledge and society. So instead they adopted a policy of non-interference; and they disguised themselves as Earthlings so they could study Earthling ways in secret.

They also went to great lengths to keep their discovery from the Verdissians, who had already stolen their wormhole technology. Yet, despite the Ceruleans' best efforts, the secret of Earth's existence had somehow got out. Snipper wondered if they had been followed through the wormhole or perhaps even had a traitor in their midst. But it was a sensitive subject, and no one wanted to talk about it.

In any case, by the end of the week, all conversation was at an end. The crew had put on an impressive amount of weight. Hibernival was brought to an official close with one last enormous feast. Then all the Ceruleans got up and marched off to the hibernation deck. Snipper was alone.

Chapter Six

In the course of his journey through the wormhole, Snipper spent far longer alone than he had ever done before. And he quickly discovered that the Ceruleans had not given him the run of the place after all: indeed, they had sealed off the majority of their spaceship, effectively locking him in the living quarters. He could very easily have felt claustrophobic. But, as a secret agent, he had been trained to cope with imprisonment in harsh conditions - including isolation from his fellow hedgehogs. This at least was no prison. He had all the creature comforts. He also had more than enough to keep himself occupied.

His first priority was to learn Cerulean. Despite his natural gift for languages, he had picked up very little indeed. But he had received no encouragement from the crew. Whatever method they themselves had used to become so fluent in Earthling languages over so short a period, they did not share with him. Perhaps they considered their language too difficult for a simple Earthling. Or perhaps they preferred to exclude him from their private conversations.

Naturally, there was no such thing as *Teach Yourself Cerulean* available on his holographic device. But he soon discovered how to toggle between languages. This gave him a set of parallel texts to work from - both written and sung. For several weeks, he seldom had his

nose out of his holographic books. And, by the fifth week, he had worked out the basics of their language.

Using Cerulean search terms, he now found many more books on his holographic device than had been available to him before. He picked out two as being of particular interest. The first was *The Complete Spaceship Manual*, which explained the workings of every type of Cerulean spacecraft currently in service. The second was *Teach Yourself Verdissian: Learning by Osmosis.* Snipper hesitated here. Learning a language through its unconscious absorption seemed a little too optimistic. On the other hand, the Ceruleans had become fluent in Earthly languages in just six months. So he decided to give it a go. Putting on a headset, he quickly discovered it served a dual purpose - delivering not only sound but also a small electrical charge. Though a little startling at first, the feeling was not unpleasant, and Snipper soon realized this faint electrical pulse was actually improving his ability to learn.

In the meantime, his understanding of the Cerulean language also continued to improve. And, as soon as it was good enough, he started reading the spaceship manual. He quickly identified the *ISV Resurgence* as a C2 class ISV - an interstellar space vehicle capable of travelling through wormholes, though unable to land; while the smaller spacecraft they had arrived in was a K1 spacelander, which could land but was not wormhole-enabled. Snipper studied the main systems of both - everything from engines and solar wind sails to manoeuvring and navigation systems.

It was while he was mugging up on the layout of the C2 that he discovered the process for shutting one deck off from another - and opening them up again. He almost dropped the holographic device in his excitement. Rushing over to the exit, he waved his paw in a figure of eight. Then, speaking out loud in his best Cerulean, he commanded the doors to open. They immediately glided apart. As he left the living quarters, he felt like a hoglet let loose in a sweetshop - after everyone else had gone home. Despite the drop in temperature, he was far too excited to go back for his coat. And, on re-entering the weightless zone, he did a couple of somersaults - just because he could.

His first stop was the hibernation deck. Stepping inside, he noticed a further fall in temperature. A long, narrow, dimly-lit space, it was lined on every side with pods - hundreds of them. Inside each pod, visible through a sealed glass door, there floated a single hedgehog. Freed from the restriction of clothes, they were curled up tight - as

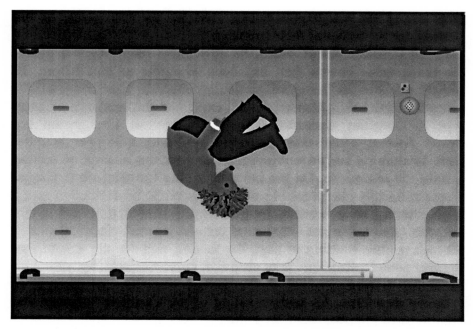

nature had intended. Yet this scene was about as far from nature as it was possible to be. In a natural environment, hibernation can be a risky business: unconscious hedgehogs cannot defend themselves from attack and, if temperatures fall too low, they must wake up and seek shelter elsewhere. But, here on the spaceship, everything was closely controlled by computers. Inside each pod was a sensor; outside was a thermometer giving a reading equivalent to 1° centigrade. According to the *Spaceship Manual*, this was the ideal temperature for hibernation - though it was three degrees lower than the ideal for any Earthling to hibernate. No doubt the Ceruleans had evolved differently on their chilly planet.

Snipper shivered. This was no place for a fully conscious Earthling with no coat. So he moved on quickly to the simulator room. As a qualified aeroplane pilot, he could not resist the opportunity to learn to fly a spacelander and an ISV. Indeed, from now on, he spent half his waking hours either mugging up on his *Spaceship Manual* or practising in the simulators. Though the ISV required a large crew, the simulator was completely flexible. Snipper could take on any role he wished, while the remaining roles were taken on by a virtual crew. One-by-one, he worked through every function. He learned to manoeuvre the spaceship, changing speed or direction; and he learnt how to search for, stabilize and expand a wormhole. By contrast, the spacelander could be flown by a single hedgehog, and had no wormhole technology to master. In this machine, Snipper taught himself to dock, undock, fly, land and take off. With so much to learn, the days quickly turned into weeks. And, before he knew it, the weeks became months.

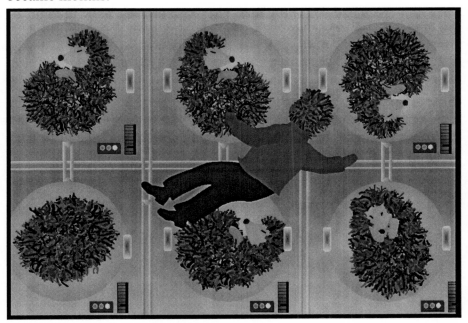

Chapter Seven

When Despina came to, there were three green hedgehogs in fancy dress standing before her. Unable to believe what she saw, she pinched herself and then rubbed her eyes. But nothing changed. The hedgehogs were still green and definitely real. They also seemed to be murmuring tunefully to each other; but, on seeing Despina awake, they stopped.

"Tell us, Despina," demanded the one with the star-shaped badge on her uniform. "Where is Frau Klanger?"

"Frau Klanger?" repeated Despina. "Oh, you mean the music director at the Palace Museum. She's ill. I suppose she must... Hold on a moment, where am *I*? And who are *you*?" Despina tried to get up but the room began to swim. Feeling horribly spaced out, she sank back down into her seat again.

"You're on our spaceship. I'm afraid we had no alternative but to bring you with us. I'm Minty, the ship's captain. These are Dr Peridot and my head of intelligence, Commander Moss."

Despina stared at them. This had to be some sort of practical joke. Yet who would play such an unpleasant trick? No one she knew. Peering at them, she was half relieved to find they were, indeed, strangers. But now she was gripped by a sudden fear, for it finally dawned on her that she had been kidnapped.

How had it happened? She tried to stay calm and think back. The last thing she could remember was standing in her dressing room, practising a tricky passage from Sharp's Quartet in A flat. Somehow, she had got from there to here without knowing it. The only explanation was that she had been drugged. No doubt that accounted for her dizziness.

But why? Why had they abducted her and why had they dressed themselves up as extra-terrestrials of all things? They had gone to an awful lot of trouble; even the room seemed to have been set up to look like a spaceship. If only they had been more normal, she might have felt less afraid. But perhaps that was the point - perhaps they *wanted* to frighten her.

"You were about to tell us where Frau Klanger is," said Commander Moss.

"I don't know where she is - I've never even met her," said Despina. "Anyway, why would I tell *you*?"

"Because we're her friends," said Captain Minty. "You can trust us."

"Her friends? Really! And you expect me to trust you!" The idea of Frau Klanger having friends like these was so absurd it almost made Despina laugh. "I can tell you one thing," she said pointedly. "If I ever do meet Frau Klanger, I'll suggest she trades you in for some better ones."

"There's no point denying your connection with her," said Moss, with a note of impatience in his voice. "When we heard you playing our evacuation melody, we left the concert and went to look for her. We found this note from you in her office." Moss passed Despina a scrap of paper.

Dear Frau Klanger, it read, *I received your message this morning and have persuaded the others to play your evacuation melody. I hope it has the desired effect. Stay safe – all of you. Your friend, Despina.*

"When we found this note, there was no sign of Klanger herself," explained Moss. "Which is why we went to see you. And, while we waited for you in your dressing room, we found the original message from our friend." Moss passed Despina a second scrap of paper.

Dear Despina, it read, *my friends and I are in great danger and must evacuate immediately. It's too risky for me to warn the others using the normal channels of communication, as these have been compromised. But they're all coming to the concert tonight so, if you will play our special melody, they'll know what to do. Please do not fail us. Our safety rests in your paws. Your friend, Frau Klanger.*

71

Despina stared at the two notes, utterly perplexed. Her head felt woozier than ever. Why would her kidnappers want to fake a correspondence between her and Frau Klanger? Nothing about these hedgehogs made any sense.

"This is nonsense!" she exclaimed crossly. "This note that's meant to be from me - it isn't even in my writing!"

"Yet you did play our special melody, just as Frau Klanger asked you to do," said Moss, accusingly. "And you knew it would trigger our departure from Earth. Why did Klanger want us to evacuate? What was this danger she spoke of? Why didn't she just come to the concert?"

Despina wondered whether she should just tell them what they wanted to hear. Perhaps then they would let her go. But what exactly did they want to hear?

"Come now," said Minty. "You must know. Klanger clearly confided in you."

"How exactly? Given we've never met!" retorted Despina. "I told you, she's ill. It wasn't even her that invited me to perform at the Palace Museum."

"Who did ask you, Despina?" It was Dr Peridot who spoke now. She spoke gently, with none of Moss's impatience or Minty's briskness.

"Count de Poynte," said Despina, "Frau Klanger's temporary replacement while she was off sick."

"Did *he* tell you to play the evacuation melody?" asked Peridot.

"It was his idea to include the piece by Niemandt. But it's a perfectly normal piece of music. And we agreed to play it because we liked it - not because it contained some sort of coded message for a bunch of nutcases."

The words were no sooner spoken than regretted. Despina knew it was foolish to be so rude to her captors. The three green hedgehogs frowned and then murmured tunefully to each other. It was almost as though they were communicating through song. But who had ever heard of such a thing? Perhaps the drug they had given her had done something to her mind.

"Despina," said Minty at last, "that piece of music was not composed by any Earthling, as you must surely know. Indeed, I don't suppose there is any composer by the name of Niemandt."

"Of course there is!" protested Despina. In truth, she had never heard of Niemandt until Count de Poynte had mentioned him. But so what? Why was she letting them interrogate her anyway? She was the one who should be demanding answers. "Now I've got some questions for you," she said. She got up from her chair and actually found she was a little steadier on her feet than before. "First and foremost I want to know exactly why you've kidnapped me."

"It was not our wish to take you," said Moss. "But Frau Klanger had disappeared and you refused to tell us anything when we questioned you on Earth. Our departure had already been delayed too long. We could hardly hang around after you'd triggered an emergency evacuation. We had no choice but to bring you with us."

"But, if you answer our questions now," said Minty, "you'll be free to live out your life as you wish on our planet."

"On the other hand," said Moss, with a note of menace in his voice, "if we discover you've betrayed or in any way harmed Frau Klanger, you'll have to answer for it in a court of law."

Had Despina really believed she was on a Verdissian spaceship, she would no doubt have been deeply shocked by the alternatives now laid before her. Instead, she was more struck by Moss's claim that they had questioned her before. Thinking back to the concert interval, she now remembered there had been three hedgehogs waiting for her in her dressing room. They had been perfectly normal-looking brown hedgehogs. But they had indeed asked her where Frau Klanger was and why she thought they were in danger. Despina had, of course, been unable to tell them. After they had gone, she had picked up her violin to practise. But she had played only a few bars, when she felt a sudden sharp pain in her arm. Overcome with dizziness, she had fallen to her knees. She had tried to get up but had been too unsteady. Laying her precious violin on the floor, she had grasped the edge of the table with both paws. But, before she could haul herself up, someone had grabbed her from behind. She had struggled and then what? After that, she must have passed out, for she remembered no more.

"My violin!" she exclaimed. "What happened to my violin?"

"Your violin is of no importance," said Moss unsympathetically. "You cannot return to Earth - you know too much."

Despina stared at him in horror. Though unconvinced she had ever left Earth, his words still sent a chill down her spines. Was this some sort of threat? What were they going to do with her? She made a move for the door. Moss tried to stop her; but then Minty shook her head, and she was allowed to pass. She found herself in a long windowless corridor. On the walls were numerous photographs of planets, constellations and other astronomical phenomena. Among the

photographs were several pictures of flying saucers - computer graphics, of course, but convincingly done all the same. She could not imagine why had anyone would have gone to such lengths. But she had given up trying to understand.

Instead, she took to her heels and ran. The corridor seemed to go on and on, and eventually she had to stop to catch her breath. As she did so, she caught sight of an open door. Through it, she could see Minty, Moss and Peridot. Suddenly it dawned on her that the corridor was circular and she was back where she had started. Peridot called her name.

"Despina, wait! We can see you really don't know where you are. If you come here, we'll show you."

Despina eyed them suspiciously, until curiosity and the lack of any obvious alternative made her relent. "Well?" she said, with a note of defiance still in her voice.

Peridot said nothing but simply pressed a button on the wall. A moment later an alarm sounded over the loudspeaker system and Despina began to get an odd feeling, as though she were on a travelator. Then another more extraordinary sensation took over: she was floating. They all were.

"What have you done to me?" she cried fiercely, convinced she was hallucinating.

"We've turned off the gravity-simulator," said Peridot. "But, if that's not enough to convince you, you'd better come through here. Come on - we've got something to show you."

Taking Despina by the paw, Peridot led her across the corridor into another room. Here, the window occupied an entire wall. The view was indistinguishable from that in the first room and not so different to the night sky as seen from Earth, but for one thing. In the middle of it all was Earth itself.

Finally, the truth dawned upon Despina. She was on a spaceship, surrounded by aliens. Somewhere amid her horror, she registered the beauty of her planet and the extraordinary privilege of seeing it as few had done before. But any sense of wonder was far surpassed by her sense of desolation. For whatever reason, these extra-terrestrial hedgehogs had taken her away from everything she knew and everyone she loved. And, no matter what she said, they would not take her back. Her life as she knew it had ended.

"Are you all right?" asked Peridot. She put a sympathetic paw on Despina's shoulder. "You're shaking!"

"Am I?" murmured Despina.

"She's in shock, Captain. I should take her to sick bay."

"Very well," said Minty, "but let us know as soon as she's better so we can continue the interrogation."

75

Peridot reactivated the gravity simulator and whisked Despina off to sick bay for a full check-up. Having confirmed her diagnosis, she gave Despina a warm blanket, hot drink and – most importantly of all - some time to herself.

Alone at last, Despina's thoughts returned to friends and family. Gradually, the shock deadened and the terror subsided into a calmer sort of fear. But the sense of loss only deepened. The thought that she would never see her parents again was more painful than she could bear. Her brother, her cousins, her friends, Snipper... They were all gone from her life forever. The loss of Snipper should perhaps have been the easiest to bear, for she had known him less than a year. But instead she felt cheated. After all they had been through together, they had become very close. To be separated so soon... But no - why should she accept any of this? Even if she could not persuade these green hedgehogs to take her back, there had to be other ways. She could hijack a spaceship and force them to fly her home. She could hide and catch a lift as a stowaway. Of course, it would not be easy. It might take years - or even the rest of her life. But she *had* to try, even if it killed her in the process.

"How are you feeling?" It was Peridot, who had returned - far too quickly, in Despina's opinion.

"All right," said Despina, with a non-committal shrug of her shoulders. Peridot appeared sympathetic, but Despina was in no mood to make friends with the hedgehogs who had taken everything from her. "Why've you brought me here - on your spaceship?" she asked. "You don't really think I was exchanging messages with Frau Klanger, do you?"

"We did think that," said Peridot, "and, I'm afraid, some of us still do."

"But do *you* believe me?"

Peridot nodded. "Yes, I believe you. And the others will too, eventually. But I'm afraid Moss likes to be thorough – he does his interrogations by the book, leaving no stone unturned. All the same, I think it's about time we answered some of *your* questions. So what do you want to know?"

"Everything - starting with where you're from and exactly what you were doing on my planet. I assume Frau Klanger is one of you?"

"She is - her real name's Lieutenant Kloraphyll, and we're Verdissians. Our planet - Verdis - is located in an outer arm of the Pinwheel galaxy."

"The Pinwheel Galaxy!" exclaimed Despina. "But that's..." She had been about to protest that this was twenty million light years from Earth and that it was impossible for anyone to cover such a distance. But an hour ago she had been unable to accept she was on a spaceship, surrounded by aliens. Who was she to doubt anything now?

"You were just about to say it's too far to travel," said Peridot. "And you'd be right, ordinarily speaking. But, just over twenty years ago, we learnt how to stabilize and expand wormholes. That meant - "

"You could travel anywhere in the universe!" exclaimed Despina. As a scientist, she was familiar with the concept of wormholes, but no Earthling had yet proven their existence, let alone used them to travel vast distances.

"Exactly," said Peridot. "A new age of exploration suddenly opened up. Until then we'd been limited to our own solar system; and, though there are eighteen planets orbiting our sun, only two support life - Verdis and Cerulea."

"Two!" exclaimed Despina, astonished there were so many.

"Yes. Cerulea has a much harsher environment than Verdis or Earth," continued Peridot, "but somehow life evolved there too - sophisticated, intelligent life. Indeed, the blue hedgehogs who inhabit Cerulea were already technologically very advanced when we came upon them. Much more so than Earth. But politically and morally... Well, I'm afraid their behaviour leaves something to be desired."

"I don't suppose they go around kidnapping hedgehogs from other planets," said Despina pointedly.

"That's why we kept the secret of wormhole travel from them," said Peridot, ignoring Despina's barbed remark. "We didn't believe they'd use the knowledge responsibly."

"Unlike yourselves," murmured Despina, who was finding it difficult to hold her tongue.

"When we discovered how to harness wormholes," persisted Peridot, "we used this gift to seek out new worlds. We wanted to know whether there was life outside our own solar system - whether there existed even the right conditions for life. For many years, we explored the universe searching for the tell-tale signs of oxygen and methane. We found nothing. That is, until six months ago, when we discovered a planet whose atmosphere contained not only those gases but CFCs too. That meant intelligent life, in the early stages of technological development. We'd stumbled upon Earth."

"I see," said Despina thoughtfully. "So what exactly have you been doing on Earth for the last six months?"

"Well, our mission was to find out as much as we could about Earth - both the planet and its inhabitants. As I'm sure you can understand, it's a subject of huge scientific and academic interest to us. And, in time, we would have sent intelligence officers all over your world. But so far it's just been the four of us - Captain Minty, Commander Moss, Lieutenant Kloraphyll and me. We formed a small advance party who went to live in Hedgermany to see how well we could fit in with the local population. Each of us had a different area of interest. Captain Minty's brief was to learn about Earthling space science - "

"Then why not go to the United Stakes? They've got the biggest space programme."

"We wanted to visit a country with more history. In any case, Hedgermany's got a very interesting and varied space programme - its space lab control centre, astronaut training facility, the development of space robotics and rocket engines... You see, we did do our research. Before we landed, we spent several weeks scanning Earth's online newspapers, government websites and Priklipedia. In the end, we all agreed Hedgermany was our number-one choice. It's peaceful, stable and prosperous - all of which was essential for our very first visit to Earth; and, more than that, it's one of the world's most influential democracies. We were also rather excited by its musical history – for what other country on Earth has produced so many great classical composers?"

"So then what?" prodded Despina. "What did you do next?"

"We found jobs. Captain Minty got a temporary position in the space lab control centre, just outside Milchnicht. She also visited the astronaut training facility in western Hedgermany for a few weeks and had a very interesting time there - she even got to meet the next lot of astronauts going up to your space station."

Despina was astonished. Pawline and Schnüffel had met an alien without knowing it. But she said nothing. She feared that, if she admitted to any kind of connection with an astronaut - or anything space-related at all, it might somehow arouse suspicion.

"What about the rest of you?" she asked.

"Kloraphyll - as you know - became music director at the Palace Museum under the name Frau Klanger. I got myself a job in a hospital genetics lab so I could study Earthling DNA. And Commander Moss went to work in a newspaper, reporting on current affairs."

"And what did you make of us Earthlings?" asked Despina. "I suppose you consider us backwards."

"Yes and no," said Peridot. "Certainly your science and technology are fairly basic by Verdissian standards. Your space programmes, for example, are clearly in their infancy - several centuries behind our own. But, politically and culturally... Well, it's difficult to give a simple answer - your world is so diverse. Hedgermany certainly shows promise, as do a number of countries. But then there are other places on Earth which leave a lot to be desired. All I can really say is there's good and there's bad."

"That's fair," admitted Despina, "and no doubt you've learnt a lot. But you could have made things a lot simpler for yourselves if you'd just been honest about who you were. I don't know how you managed that trick of turning yourselves brown and learning our languages so well, but why even bother? Why disguise yourselves at all?"

"The trick, as you call it, was simply to drink a special chemical solution. It only takes a couple of days to change colour. Then, so long as you top up regularly, you can stay that way for up to nine months before you start developing any resistance to it. And learning languages is easy if you use our osmotic method -"

"Osmotic?" repeated Despina.

"Yes, the electrically stimulated unconscious absorption of knowledge. As for being open and honest, we tried that once before, when we first landed on Cerulea. We were then perhaps only fifty or sixty years ahead of the Ceruleans, technologically and scientifically speaking, but the gap was big enough to have a distorting effect upon them. They soon lost all interest in their own research and instead focussed their efforts on stealing ours. When we discovered your planet, we were determined not to make the same mistake twice. We wished to study the Earth, not alter it."

"If that was the case, how could you have believed that Frau Klanger - I mean, Frau Kloraphyll or whatever she's called - would have confided in me?"

"Because of the notes between the two of you."

"Except they're *both* fakes. Not just the one that's meant to be from me. Your friend would never have sent such a message to a complete stranger. I certainly never saw it until you showed it to me."

"The question then," said Peridot, "is who *did* write those notes. What did you say was the name of that hedgehog who asked you to play the evacuation piece - you know, the piece of music supposedly by Niemandt? It was an aristocratic name, wasn't it?"

"Count de Poynte," said Despina slowly, for a terrible thought was taking shape in her mind. "And I must admit, now I think about it, I don't really know anything about him at all. I suppose you could say he sort of came out of the blue..."

Chapter Eight

Pawline paced up and down impatiently, tapping a claw against the small tin clasped in her paws. She had found the tin in a packet left at the railway station for her by Snipper. Inside there had been five brown spines; apparently these belonged to Count de Poynte, the music director at the Palace Museum. Somehow, Snipper had got it into his head that de Poynte was from outer space. Pawline had not known whether to laugh or cry when she got Snipper's message. She feared Despina's disappearance must have affected his mind. She had tried calling and texting him; but his phone was either switched off or out of range. Now it felt as though *two* of her friends had vanished from the face of the earth.

In her desperation, Pawline had gone to Schnüffel with the tin. Asking him to perform a DNA test had been embarrassing, to say the least. She had always prided herself on being down-to-earth. But Snipper had appealed to her as a friend, and she would not let him down. Unsurprisingly, Schnüffel's response had been a polite but firm 'no'. He had tried to persuade Pawline they would be better off devoting their time to searching for their friends. But, even as they were discussing the matter, the little clutch of spines lying in the tin had gradually changed from brown to blue. And, when Schnüffel saw

what had happened, he no longer felt able to refuse. He was a scientist through and through and, though the change of colour was in no way proof of Snipper's story, it demanded an explanation.

Pawline looked at her watch. Schnüffel had been examining the data from the test for three hours now, but it seemed more like a day. She wondered why she felt so uneasy about the results. She already knew what the outcome would be: it would prove conclusively that de Poynte was no more an alien than Snipper. ...Yet Schnüffel himself had said that life was bound to exist on other planets. Certainly, if it did not, it seemed like an awful waste of space. And why not intelligent life? Why not creatures like themselves? Pawline shook her head. Even if intelligent life did exist on other planets, no extra-terrestrial would ever be visiting Earth. The distances involved were simply too great.

"Pawline," said Schnüffel, breaking his long silence at last.

"What is it?" she asked. She stopped pacing and looked him in the eye, scarcely able to breathe as she waited for him to speak. "What have you found?"

"Snipper was..." Schnüffel spoke falteringly. There was a note of reluctance in his voice. "Snipper was telling the truth. These spines don't belong to any inhabitant of Earth."

"But you're saying they're definitely real?" responded Pawline, unable to believe her ears.

"Oh yes, they're real enough. It's life, Pawline, but not as we know it."

Pawline stared at Schnüffel, dumbfounded.

For a moment, Schnüffel stared back, equally unable to believe what he, himself, had said. Then he pulled himself together. "We should report this immediately," he said. Suddenly business-like, he was now swapping his lab coat for his jacket.

"But who to?" asked Pawline. "Snipper said we should tell the space agency. But do you think they'd hear us out?"

"That depends on who we speak to there. It'll have to be someone we know well - someone who really trusts us."

"Well, nobody's going to believe a rookie like me," said Pawline modestly. "It'll have to be someone *you* know."

"Hmm," said Schnüffel thoughtfully. "How about Kratzer?"

"Oh, yes, Kratzer!" said Pawline. "You trained together, didn't you? And didn't he head up the space lab control centre here during your last mission?"

"That's right. We spoke to each other nearly every day for six months."

"Well then, he should know you pretty well by now."

Schnüffel felt that something so unbelievable could only be explained convincingly face-to-face. So they drove the twenty miles to Kratzer's house, making it there in just under thirty minutes. Much to Schnüffel's relief, Kratzer was not only at home but actually believed what he had to say about the DNA test. Pawline then filled him in on Snipper and Despina.

After that, the message passed swiftly up the ranks of the International Space Agency and, from there, out to the governments of the world. Within twenty-four hours, an emergency meeting had been called. Presidents and prime ministers from every corner of the globe, their military commanders and the International Space Agency's most senior officials all dropped what they were doing to attend. Unable to agree an immediate course of action, they talked late into the night and on into the following morning. Many were concerned by just how little solid information they possessed. Some noted that no formal offer of protection had yet been made by the Ceruleans. Indeed, the only indication of a Verdissian threat so far was the abduction of a single hedgehog; the suggestion that the Verdissians would return to launch a full-scale slave trade from Earth was mere opinion. Others pointed out that the only real evidence of the aliens' existence was five blue spines. So more scientists were brought in and they repeated Schnüffel's DNA test - again and again. The result was always the same.

Schnüffel and Pawline were, of course, questioned at length. Beyond that, however, the matter was out of their paws; there was nothing further they could do for their friends. For a while, they wondered if their mission would be cancelled. On the contrary, the International Space Agency was keener than ever to send them up. And, for the very first time, arms and ammunition were loaded onto the space shuttle. In the event of an alien invasion, the space station would become Earth's first line of defence. Not that anyone believed the station could hold out for long. Its multi-layered casing shielded it from micrometeoroids; but it was not designed to withstand a prolonged armed attack. Indeed, if the casing were penetrated, the astronauts would have no hope of survival. But the symbolic importance of the space station was felt to be too great for the astronauts to surrender without resistance.

It was therefore with mixed feelings that Pawline and Schnüffel flew to the United Stakes to begin their period of quarantine prior to launch. The purpose of the quarantine was to isolate the astronauts from any germs before they flew into space. For there was no hospital on board the space station, and the astronauts themselves had only basic medical training. Most of them appreciated the time in quarantine. They valued the opportunity to rest and relax before a strenuous mission, free from distractions and responsibilities. But on this occasion relaxation was not so easy. All members of the crew had now been fully briefed on the possible threat of an alien invasion. A feeling of unease hung in the air. Space travel was, of course, risky by its very nature. The astronauts knew and accepted that. But this was a different sort of danger – unexpected, ill-understood and impossible to prepare for.

As for Pawline, during the quarantine her thoughts often returned to her missing friends. She thought wistfully of their promise to attend her launch. In Snipper's case, she had never really believed he would make it. He had so often dropped out of things at the last minute and offered only the feeblest of excuses. But to say this was different would be a monumental understatement. For it now seemed that Snipper had hidden depths. Until recently, she had never thought of him as especially brave. Yet, without any kind of preparation, he had boldly gone where no hedgehog from Earth had gone before. He must surely have been afraid. Yet, for Despina's sake, he had overcome this. Pawline feared she would never see either of them again. But, eventually, she forced herself to stop thinking about them. For she too was going into space and she needed to be completely focussed on her own mission.

It was nine o'clock in the morning, four hours before lift-off, when Pawline, Schnüffel and their five fellow astronauts finally departed for the launch pad. As they left Crew Quarters, they were greeted by the cheers of the waiting crowd. Photographers clicked furiously, trying to capture the moment. The astronauts' families shouted their goodbyes, waving flags and paws aloft. Pawline spotted her own family and waved back. Then the astronauts boarded the astro-van and were driven the three miles to the launch pad.

As they stepped out onto the tarmac, Pawline looked up at the shuttle in awe. Stood on its tail, the winged orbiter towered above them. Taller still were the twin rocket boosters and external tank which would help blast the orbiter into space. As the shuttle creaked and steam swirled around its base, it occurred to Pawline that it was really just a large aeroplane strapped onto a huge missile. But she was too thrilled to feel much afraid. Indeed, as they took the lift up to Level 195, she could hardly stop smiling. At the top, she paused to look at the view across the plain. Two miles away, the spectators were gathering, her family among them. With a few minutes to spare, she called them to say a final goodbye. Then she walked across to the ante-room, where the Closeout Crew helped her into her harness, powered her space suit and checked all her equipment. Ready to go now, she got down on all fours and crawled through the side hatch into the cockpit, where another member of the Closeout Crew was waiting for her. She climbed up into her seat, and he strapped her in.

When all the astronauts were aboard, there were still many tasks to be performed - everything from checking air-to-ground voice communications to activating flight recorders and testing space suits and helmets for leaks. But, eventually, the preparations were complete. The Closeout Crew said their goodbyes and locked the hatch. Listening through her headphones, Pawline heard Launch Control give the countdown.

We have go for auto sequence start. T-20 seconds and counting... 15 seconds... 9, 8, 7... We have go for main engines start...

The shuttle's three main engines were now lit. There was a low rumble. Then the cockpit began to vibrate.

3, 2, 1... continued the countdown. *Booster ignition and lift-off!*

As the solid rocket boosters were lit, the low rumble became a roar. The cockpit was shaking violently now. A moment later, the bolts pinning the shuttle to the launch pad were blown off, and the astronauts were catapulted upwards. The shuttle was now accelerating at a phenomenal rate, pinning the astronauts down hard in their seats. Then it twisted and turned onto its back. A few seconds later, flames shot over the windows: the solid rocket boosters were being jettisoned. As they separated from the shuttle, the astronauts were thrown forwards. For a minute it felt as though they were plummeting back down to Earth. Then very gradually the shuttle began to accelerate again, until the pressure was even more intense than before. Passing the eight-minute mark at a speed of 3,400 miles per hour, the pressure became almost unbearable. But then quite suddenly it stopped and they were free-floating: the main engines had been cut off. Pawline saw the external tank pass the window as it fell back to Earth. Then there was one last shove, a flash of light and a noise which sounded as though the back of the orbiter had been blown off. The next moment, there was utter peace, complete silence and the magic of weightlessness. They were in orbit.

Part Two
Chapter Nine

It was Snipper's 101st Earth-day alone when the warmth finally returned to the whole spaceship. Snipper was in the ISV simulator when it happened, in the middle of stabilizing a virtual wormhole. Indeed, he was so focussed on this tricky manoeuvre that he did not immediately notice the rising temperature. But, when he did, he knew exactly what it meant. The crew were coming out of hibernation.

Snipper had prepared for this moment. He knew that, after several months of unconsciousness, a hedgehog might normally be expected to take three or four hours to wake up. But the Ceruleans' highly controlled environment would undoubtedly speed everything up - perhaps even halving the time it would take for them to become active. Based upon his calculations, he reckoned he should have at least an hour to return to the living quarters. This was plenty of time to close up and remove all traces of his visit. Nevertheless, he was not going to hang around. He immediately unstrapped himself from his seat - leaving the virtual wormhole to collapse in upon itself and destroy the virtual spaceship. Then he wiped the simulator's memory, switched the machine off and propelled himself towards the door. His final act was to wipe the CCTV footage of his secret visits to the weightless zone.

When eventually the Ceruleans started to emerge, they found Snipper sitting quietly in the living quarters, reading the *Encyclopaedia of the Universe*. No one suspected for a moment that he had visited them on the hibernation deck, learnt to fly their spaceship and taught himself their language.

When Cyanne found him, she took him to the observation deck to watch the exit from the wormhole. For a while, they just floated around the glass dome, watching the streams of light and dust encircle them. Then the spaceship began to vibrate, just as it had done when they entered the wormhole. A moment later there was a flash of light, followed by the blackness which Snipper recognized as the wormhole horizon. Then gradually stars began to appear. At first they were just faint pinpricks of light, but little by little they grew brighter. Snipper had not seen a single star for more than three months. For a brief moment, it almost felt like a homecoming. But, of course, it was not. These were not the familiar constellations seen from Earth's solar system. And the misty grey-green planet in front of them was most definitely not Earth.

"That's Verdis," announced Cyanne.

"It's beautiful," said Snipper.

"Yes, but Earth is more beautiful."

Cyanne spoke almost longingly. Snipper was surprised she should

have such strong feelings about his planet. Then he remembered their last glimpse of Earth - a bright blue sphere encircled with swirls of white cloud. It *was* hard to imagine anything more lovely.

"Will the Verdissians know we're here?" he asked.

"They'll know someone's here, but not that it's us - we've deployed our holographic cloak. Mind you," she added, glancing at the device strapped to her wrist, "we're still 1.4 light seconds away - that's just over 260,000 miles to you. So we're well within interplanetary space and wouldn't be expected to identify ourselves anyway."

Shortly after their exit from the wormhole, Snipper learnt that Captain Cobalt had been in contact with the Cerulean High Command. Woad now received official approval for all his previous dealings with Snipper. Not only was the policy of non-interference scrapped, but the Cerulean Space Force was placed on alert, ready to offer Earth its protection. Meanwhile Snipper was encouraged to photograph and film the *ISV Resurgence* and its crew. This was for the benefit of any Earthlings who, following his return, might still be reluctant to believe in the existence of extra-terrestrials. Last but not least, the plan to rescue Despina was given the go-ahead. Back on board the *Resurgence*, a meeting was called to discuss the plan. Attending were Captain Cobalt, Commander Woad, most of the Earth landing party and Snipper. The meeting was opened by Woad, who spoke in Hedgerman so Snipper would understand.

"Welcome, everyone," he began. "I'm glad to report the situation on the ground's looking good. We now know Despina's exact location. She's being held in a low security facility in Viridian. That's on the Light Side, Snipper, so we shan't be going in under cover of darkness - but, don't worry, we'll be disguised as Verdissians."

"What about the spacelander?" asked Snipper. "Won't they realize it's not one of theirs?"

"Oh no," said Flight Lieutenant Azziur, "the spacelander will be disguised, as well. I'll deploy a holographic cloak as we approach; the Verdissians will believe it's one of their own."

"So, tell me Woad," said Captain Cobalt. "How do you plan to get into the facility where they're holding Despina?"

"Through our Verdissian contact, sir. In return for a generous payment, Major Grass has secretly provided us with transfer papers for Despina and passes for ourselves. So all we have to do is turn up at the front door. Then we walk off again, taking Despina with us.

Everything's in place. We'll be ready to go in two Earth days - as soon as our disguises are ready."

"And what if there's trouble?"

"I don't expect any, sir. But we'll be armed."

"I take it you'll be leading the rescue party, yourself?"

"Yes, sir. I want to keep it small-scale. So it'll just be Lappis, Lazzuli and me. Azziur and Sapphire will remain in the spacelander with Snipper."

"What?" said Snipper, who had not travelled halfway across the universe only to be left behind now. "No, no, I'm coming with you."

"Out of the question!" said Woad sternly. "You'd just get in the way. Surely you don't want to put Despina at risk simply to satisfy your curiosity?"

Snipper was indignant. His curiosity had nothing to do with it. He was a highly trained secret agent with plenty of experience in undercover operations. Yet he could hardly say so. "Look, I used to be in the army," he lied, "so I've done this sort of thing before. What's more, Despina knows and trusts me."

Before Woad could respond, Captain Cobalt cut in; but now he was speaking Cerulean. Snipper pricked up his ears, straining to understand while retaining a look of blank incomprehension on his face.

"Do you really plan to leave Snipper behind, Woad? You don't think it looks a little odd after you've brought him all this way?"

"We must, sir," replied Woad in Cerulean. "It's too risky to take him with us. We'd have no control over what he sees."

"But if you leave him behind," said Cobalt, "you risk losing his goodwill. He may even become suspicious. Look, why don't you take Cyanne with you? She can make sure he sees nothing - keep an eye on him while the rest of you focus on the mission."

"Very well, sir," said Woad. "Cyanne, you'll need to sort out disguises for Snipper and yourself."

Snipper was now thoroughly alarmed, though he worked hard not to show it. All his early suspicions about Woad came flooding back. Had he been responsible for Despina's kidnapping after all?

"Sir?" interjected Cyanne. "I don't understand - what mustn't Snipper see?"

"He mustn't see Despina being killed," said Captain Cobalt.

Snipper felt sick. He wondered whether he had misunderstood. Perhaps his grasp of the Cerulean language was not as good as he thought.

"Killed, sir?" repeated Cyanne. She looked upset.

"Yes," replied Woad, without any trace of emotion. "Before we leave Verdis, fighting will break out and Despina will die. If we're very lucky, she may even be killed in the crossfire. Otherwise, I'll deliver the fatal shot myself. Either way, we shall blame her death on the Verdissians."

Now Snipper could scarcely contain his feelings - let alone hide them. For a few seconds, his face betrayed him: anyone who had looked now would see he had understood every word. But all eyes were on Cyanne - whose own wide-eyed astonishment showed that she, at least, had known nothing of this murderous plot.

"But, sir, why do you want to kill Despina?" she asked.

"Because by now she's likely to know the truth about the Verdissians. If she's allowed to live and go home with Snipper - if they discover we've lied to them, they'll turn their fellow Earthlings against us before we've even started. Worse still, if they work out what we're planning, they may even ask for Verdissian protection; and *that* would mean the end of everything. Despina's death, on the other hand, will strengthen our position - it'll provide proof of Verdissian brutality. When Snipper returns to Earth with his friend's body, he'll be able to show his fellow Earthlings what the Verdissians are capable of. Earth will soon be crying out for *our* protection."

"Excuse me, sir," said Cyanne nervously, "but aren't *we* being brutal if we kill Despina?"

"We're being realistic," responded Woad sternly. "Any loss of life is regrettable, of course, but these Earthlings aren't our equals - you mustn't equate their suffering with ours. And *we* have suffered long enough. Don't forget, in the long term, the Earthlings stand to benefit almost as much as we do. Despina won't have died in vain."

"Yes, sir. Of course, sir," said Cyanne quietly.

She bowed her head - whether in shame or submission, Snipper was unsure. Then there was a moment's silence, before Woad turned and spoke to Snipper in Hedgerman.

"Snipper, you'll be pleased to know that Captain Cobalt has persuaded me to take you with us after all. Space Cadet Cyanne will come too. She'll keep an eye on you and make sure you come to no harm."

"Thank you. I'm most grateful," said Snipper, trying hard to hide his true emotions.

"Good. Now we've got that sorted out, Lieutenant Lazzuli will show us the facility where they're holding Despina."

Lazzuli nodded and, squeezing a tiny remote control in his paw, made a holographic scene appear above the table. At its centre was a strange building, which looked rather like a flying saucer on stilts. It stood in a walled garden carpeted with wild flowers. The walls were of rough stone and uneven height, and the entrance was through a low gate guarded by two rather harmless-looking green hedgehogs. To describe the place as low security seemed like an understatement.

"Despina's room is on the top floor," said Lazzuli, "but she's allowed to roam freely during waking hours - as you'll see shortly. The garden perimeter is enclosed within an impenetrable force field. But, of course, this needn't concern us as we'll enter and exit through the gate. Ah, here's Despina, herself..."

Lazzuli paused as a tiny brown hedgehog emerged from the building. Instinctively, Snipper reached out his paw to touch her. She was solid - utterly lifelike, from the fur on her face to the spines on her head. He longed to pick her up - protect her - but, of course, she was just a hologram. And, a moment later, she had disappeared.

Back in his room, Snipper sank onto his bed and buried his face in his paws. Why on earth had he trusted the Ceruleans? He was an experienced secret agent, taught to trust no one. But how else could he have reached Despina in this far-flung corner of the universe, if not on their spaceship? Whatever their motives, the Ceruleans had got him here - had been the only means by which he could have got here. And it was

92

only because he had come with them that he had discovered that *they* were the real threat to Earth. In return, he had given them nothing - told them nothing. They still did not know he was a highly trained secret agent. They did not know just how thoroughly he had explored their spaceship or the hours and hours he had spent in their simulators.

But what was he to do now? If he tried to stop the Ceruleans' so-called rescue party, Despina would be left stranded on Verdis forever. On the other hand, if he let the operation go ahead, it was unlikely he could protect her. He would be outnumbered six to one. That was to say nothing of the Verdissians he would encounter along the way - for he could hardly expect any help from Despina's kidnappers. And, even if he did somehow manage to give them all the slip and rescue his friend, the two Earthlings would still be stuck on a strange planet in a far off galaxy. They would have no way of getting home and no way of warning their fellow Earthlings against the Cerulean threat.

It was clear there was far too much to think about and there were far too many unknowns. Snipper therefore decided to concentrate on saving Despina and to worry about the rest later. But, to have any hope of rescuing her, he would need help. He had seen Cyanne's reaction to the murder plot and, though she had not protested for long, he believed she could be worked upon.

Just as he was coming to this conclusion, Cyanne herself turned up in his room. She was clutching a small green bottle in her paw. As she greeted him, Snipper noticed an awkwardness in her manner, which had not been there before.

"Here, take this," she said, avoiding eye contact as she passed him the bottle. "It's *viritinctus*, a chemical solution similar to the one we took on Earth - except it turns you green not brown. Take your first dose now and then further doses at regular, five-hour intervals; and make sure you don't miss any. I'll also need your pawprint before we go."

Snipper placed the bottle on his bedside table, continuing to watch her as he did so. He tried to read her expression, but then she turned away.

"Isn't there something else you want to tell me?" he asked, his voice as cool as ice.

Cyanne hesitated for a moment and then replied without turning back: "No, I don't think so. You'll get the rest of your disguise later. I'll see you at supper."

She stepped towards the door but, before she could open it, Snipper had grabbed her wrist and spun her round. "Oh, but I think there is!"

"How dare you!" exclaimed Cyanne, struggling to be free. "Let go of me at once!"

Snipper let go. Usually so calm under pressure, he was finding it difficult to keep his feelings in check; but he was pinning all his hopes on Cyanne and knew he could not afford to alienate her.

"I just want to know what's going on," he said as calmly as he could.

"I don't know what you mean," said Cyanne nervously. "You already know what's going on - we're going to rescue Despina." Her voice trembled as she spoke. Though she was certain Snipper could not know the truth, she was troubled by a bad conscience.

"It's no use pretending, Cyanne. I know all about Woad's plot to murder her. And that *you're* the ones threatening Earth - not the Verdissians. I'm guessing you somehow tricked the Verdissians into taking Despina. What I want you to tell me is *why*."

"You know!" exclaimed Cyanne, first shocked by the discovery and then overcome with shame. "I'm sorry... I really am. I'd no idea they were planning to hurt her - not until the meeting today."

"You still agreed to help them," said Snipper sternly.

"How did you find out? Surely you couldn't have understood what was said at the meeting?"

94

"Every word, and it's obvious you had no intention of warning me. *And* you still haven't answered my question - why?"

Cyanne sank onto the sofa. "Our planet's dying," she said. "Cerulea's more than just cold. It's on the very edge of the habitable zone around our sun. Yet we've managed. More than that, we've built a great civilization. But our orbit is changing. We're travelling further and further from our sun. Within our own lifetimes we shall be cast into outer darkness."

"So you're looking for a new home," murmured Snipper.

Cyanne nodded.

"Verdis?" he asked hopefully. His heart stood still as he waited for the answer, but there was none. "So it's to be Earth then," he said at last. "You're planning to invade Earth."

"Not *invade*. We don't want bloodshed - "

"What do you call Despina's murder then?" asked Snipper between gritted teeth.

"I told you I didn't know they were planning to kill her. In any case, if it hadn't been for *your* interference, she'd have been left alone. It's only because you followed us to Igelininsel that Commander Woad decided to bring you with us. And it's only because you're with us that Despina has to die. ...But, of course, if Woad finds out you already know the truth, he'll kill you instead."

"Well, that at least is a comfort," said Snipper grimly. "But why engineer Despina's abduction in the first place? What's she got to do with your plans to invade - or should I say 'move' - to Earth?"

"We didn't engineer her abduction. We didn't even know the Verdissians would take her – it was never part of the plan. In fact, we still don't know why they did it. All we wanted was for them to leave. They'd sent a party of explorers to Hedgermany and we - "

"They're explorers then - not slave traders?"

"Well, it's all right for them," said Cyanne resentfully. "They're nice and cosy on their planet. They've no interest in Earth other than idle curiosity. *We* need a new home and we weren't going to let them stand in our way. That's why Commander Woad disguised himself as Count de Poynte and took up the post of music director at the Palace Museum. That way he could get Despina to play the Verdissians' emergency evacuation code at the concert. We knew they'd be attending and, when they heard it, they'd have to leave."

"Do I take it the Verdissians wouldn't have approved of your plans?"

"It's unlikely. But then they wouldn't have understood that we'll make Earth a better place. Your planet is disunited and disorganized. You fight among yourselves. But on Cerulea we've come together under a single government – you see, our civilization is far in advance of yours. And we shall use our experience and superior understanding to unite Earth, under a single Cerulean government."

"And what exactly would become of *us*?"

"Nothing! As I said, we've no wish to harm you. That's why Commander Woad wanted you to believe in the Verdissian threat. He hoped you'd return to Earth and persuade your fellow Earthlings to seek Cerulean protection. That would have paved the way for us to take over peacefully. But you and your fellow Earthlings will stay where you are – just working under our direction."

"So it's the Ceruleans who plan to enslave Earth!"

"Enslave's a nasty word!"

"It isn't the word that's nasty."

"But you'd *benefit* from our rule. With our superior intelligence and knowledge, and your labour, we can create prosperity throughout your planet. There'd be no more famine and no more suffering."

"No more suffering!" exclaimed Snipper, unable to believe his ears.

"Yes!" said Cyanne, her eyes alight with fervour now. She rose and started pacing up and down. "It's still not too late, Snipper. Just agree to speak for us - persuade your fellow Earthlings to submit! Then no one will have to die."

"You're out of your mind!" exclaimed Snipper angrily. "Do you really think I'd encourage the enslavement of my entire planet? Earth's *our* home, and you've no right to it."

Cyanne shook her head, apparently exasperated by Snipper's inability to see reason. "But I've read your Earthling books," she continued. "Throughout your history, the strong have conquered the weak."

"I never said we were perfect," said Snipper. "Whatever we've done among ourselves, that doesn't change the nature of right and wrong. And it's still wrong to invade another hedgehog's planet. With your superior intelligence, I should have thought you'd have understood that!"

"What about the prosperity we could offer you? The end of suffering? Don't you want that?"

"Nonsense! Why should I believe your promises? And, even if I did... Well, perhaps your idea of suffering and mine are not the same. Better by far to be poor and free than slaves."

"You mean to say you value freedom above *everything* else?"

"Don't you?"

Cyanne hesitated for a moment, as she considered the matter. "Yes, we do but we're - " She was about to say 'superior' but refrained. She was beginning to get the distinct impression that Snipper found her claims of superiority annoying. She changed tack. "And what of us? What of our dying planet?"

Snipper knew the Ceruleans could never be allowed to settle on Earth - even if they now changed their plan and asked only for a place to live alongside Earthlings as their equals. How could they ever be trusted?

"Given your extraordinary intelligence, I'm sure you'll find an alternative solution," he said unsympathetically. Then he recollected himself and changed his approach. "Listen, Cyanne, I'm sorry about your situation – I truly am, but you've got years to save your planet. I've got just two days to save my friend. So, *please*, will you help me? Surely you don't want to be an accessory to murder?"

"Of course I don't - but you can hardly expect me to betray my fellow Ceruleans - to wreck Commander Woad's plan."

"But Despina's death can serve no purpose now," responded Snipper. "Earth won't seek Cerulea's protection without my testimony."

"Maybe not," said Cyanne, "but it makes no difference - I won't fight against my own kind. In any case, even with my help, you wouldn't stand a chance."

"I'm not suggesting we fight our way out of this," said Snipper. "This so-called rescue party isn't due to leave for another two days. That gives me a good head start. And I'm not even asking you to come with me. I'll go on my own. I just need you to get some things for me."

"But you can't fly the spacelander!"

"Actually, I can. I practised in the simulator while you were hibernating."

"But how did you...?" Cyanne was lost for words. Snipper seemed to be extraordinarily resourceful for a mere Earthling. She had been astonished enough that he had managed to teach himself Cerulean. But this! Gradually, he was chipping away at her belief in Cerulean superiority. "Yes, well, that's very impressive," she said, a little reluctantly. "But what about your disguise? The *viritinctus* needs two full days to take effect. If you go early, you'll be greeny-brown."

"I was thinking I might increase the dosage," said Snipper.

Cyanne frowned. She picked up the bottle and read the directions out loud. "*If you take too much viritinctus, immediately contact your doctor or go to your nearest hospital. Symptoms of an overdose include headaches, dizziness and nausea.*"

Snipper wrinkled his nose. He had no wish to make himself ill, but it was a price worth paying for Despina's freedom. "I'll take my chances," he said, as he measured out a double dose and drank it down in one. It tasted awful. "Now, what I need from you are those Verdissian passes and transfer papers Woad mentioned. Plus two space suits, two Verdissian uniforms, an extra bottle of *viritinctus,* a couple of laser guns and a Verdissian-style backpack."

"Oh, well, if that's *all* you need..." said Cyanne sarcastically.

"I know it's a lot," said Snipper. "I wouldn't ask if there were any other way."

"I'd be taking a big risk," said Cyanne.

Snipper had no idea what would happen to Cyanne if she were caught helping him. He imagined it would not be good. But he needed her and, perhaps a little ruthlessly, hoped to take advantage of her guilty conscience. "Don't you think you owe me this?" he asked.

"Well," she said, sighing. "I'm not all happy about betraying my fellow Ceruleans… but neither will I stand by and watch them commit cold-blooded murder. So, yes, I'll get those things you've asked for. But that's it. Afterwards, I don't want to know."

"Don't worry, that's all I need... besides a little information."

"Yes?" said Cyanne warily.

"The co-ordinates for the nearest landing site, and directions to the compound where they're holding Despina."

"All right," said Cyanne. "But then that really is it."

"Thank you, Cyanne. You're a star." Snipper wanted to say more - how brave she was, how her heart was in the right place for all her Cerulean pride - but he was afraid she might take it the wrong way.

"What will you do afterwards?" she asked. "Once you've found Despina? You know the spacelander isn't equipped for wormhole travel, so it can't get you home. And, of course, returning to the *Resurgence* is out of the question."

"I know that. I'll just have to cross that bridge when I get to it - *if* I get to it. At least Despina and I will have lived to fight another day."

Chapter Ten

Cyanne got the things Snipper had asked for. Then, during sleeping hours, while the *ISV Resurgence* was on autopilot and only a skeleton crew remained on duty, the two hedgehogs made their way to the spacelander. Cyanne led the way, first checking the coast was clear. Snipper followed. When they reached the boarding chamber, they locked the door behind them, and Cyanne helped Snipper into his Verdissian space suit. Looking in the mirror, he hardly recognized himself.

"You're sure I'm green enough?" asked Snipper anxiously.

"Spot on. Indistinguishable from a Verdissian. How's your head?"

"I'll live," said Snipper. He could have done without the thumping headache brought on by his *viritinctus* overdose, but at least he had avoided the other side effects.

"Here you are - gloves, helmet, *ubikwe*."

The *ubikwe* was a small wrist-worn device with multiple functions, including altimeter and gravity sensor. Snipper put it on. Then, tucking his helmet under his arm, he grabbed his gloves and suitcase with his free paw and wriggled through the entry hatch into the spacelander. He put his suitcase in a locker and, floating over to the pilot's seat, strapped himself in. Cyanne followed with his Verdissian backpack and stowed it alongside the suitcase. The two hedgehogs then spent a rather tense thirty minutes carrying out checks. This was a vital safety precaution, but they were both anxious for Snipper to be gone. The sooner he made it into Verdissian airspace, the better. Woad would be unlikely to risk following him there when he realized he was gone and that his own murderous operation was blown.

"That's everything," said Cyanne. "You're ready to go now... though it's not too late to turn back. Are you really sure you want to go through with this?"

"Completely sure," said Snipper. "Will *you* be all right? Have you covered your tracks properly?"

"I'll be fine," said Cyanne. "I've left your holographic device on your bed, as you suggested, so they'll see what you've been reading. They'll be so focussed on how you taught yourself to fly and to speak Cerulean, I doubt they'll worry too much about how you got a few things out of storage."

"Good," said Snipper. "All the same, I couldn't have done this without you. I'm more grateful than I can possibly say..." Snipper wanted to tell Cyanne that he felt sure some way would be found to save Cerulea. But what did *he* know? And he had just persuaded her to ignore the Ceruleans' only existing plan for a new future. Any words from him on this subject would sound hollow and dishonest. So he decided it was better to say nothing.

"Goodbye, Snipper," said Cyanne. "Good luck."

"Thanks, Cyanne. And you take care of yourself."

The two hedgehogs shook paws warmly. Then Cyanne floated off through the entry hatch. Once Snipper had heard it click shut, he locked it from the inside and then waited a further fifteen minutes to give her plenty of time to return to her quarters. He wanted to be sure she was tucked up in bed before he triggered the alarm with his departure.

When the fifteen minutes were up, Snipper took a deep breath and focussed. He was about to fly a spacecraft through an alien atmosphere and land it on a hostile planet. If he had been honest with himself, he would have admitted that, deep down, he was terrified. But he was used to suppressing any feelings of fear, and right now all he registered was a faint sense of unease. He told himself the cockpit was identical to the interior of the simulator. And, though he had not spent hundreds of hours training for every conceivable eventuality, as real astronauts do, he had practised all standard procedures. So long as nothing went wrong, he would be fine.

Snipper powered up the computer systems; then he entered the composition, depth and density of the Verdissian atmosphere, the prevailing wind direction and the landing site co-ordinates. Finally he released the docking hooks and, with a quick burn of his engines, gently pushed away from the *Resurgence*. Once clear, he opened up the throttle and fired on all thrusters. The spacelander shot forward at a breath-taking speed, pinning Snipper to his seat. Within seconds, he had entered Verdissian airspace. An alarm sounded and a green light flashed, warning him to present his Verdissian pass key. He waved the card Cyanne had given him in front of the scanner, whereupon the alarm stopped and the green light went off.

Welcome to Verdissian airspace, announced a disembodied voice. *Please fly carefully around our planet.*

Snipper was keen to fly as carefully as he possibly could. The speedometer was already showing the equivalent of an incredible 205,000 miles per hour. But, at this stage, an occasional check of the automatic guidance system was enough. It would be another hour before Snipper's total concentration was required, as he entered the Verdissian atmosphere. For now, he was able to gaze out of the window, watching in fascination as Verdis grew steadily bigger. Though much of the planet was shrouded in cloud, it was not long before he began to distinguish continents and oceans. And he could hardly believe what he was seeing - a strange new world which, not so long ago, he had not even known existed.

The hour passed quickly and, all too soon, Snipper had to face up to the biggest flying challenge of his life. At an altitude of 100,000 feet, he dipped the spacelander's tail, ready for entry into the Verdissian atmosphere. Then he fired his forward thrusters. As his speed plummeted, he was thrown into his seat belt. By 92,000 feet, he was flying at just 23,140 miles per hour. This was orbital velocity - the exact speed required to stay in orbit around Verdis. But, of course, Snipper wanted to land on Verdis, not orbit it. He watched intently as his speed continued to fall. A moment later, he had passed the point of no return. Without refuelling, this was now a one-way journey.

Snipper's eyes were fixed to his computer screens. There was only a narrow corridor within which he could enter the Verdissian atmosphere safely. If he came in at too shallow an angle, the spacelander would bounce off into a low orbit from which controlled re-entry would be impossible. If he came in too steeply, the plane would not be able to withstand the heat.

Snipper certainly knew when he entered the Verdissian atmosphere, for it burst into flames all around him. The cabin was bathed in a bright orange light. All the while, his eyes remained on the monitor. Throughout the descent, the automatic guidance system made tiny adjustments to keep the lander on course. Once, as it banked less steeply than he had expected, he thought he must be just seconds from burning up. His paws hovered over the manual controls as he kept his eyes glued to the monitor. But overriding the lander's guidance system would itself be risky. Keeping his cool, he continued to watch and wait - and then breathed a sigh of relief when the lander readjusted its position.

As the spacelander continued its descent, the flames around it eventually cleared. The risk of burning up or bouncing back off into space had passed. Snipper pulled a lever, inflating the side fins at the rear of the lander into full swept-back wings: the rocket had become an aeroplane. All Snipper had to worry about now was landing a plane bigger than a jumbo jet and not getting himself shot down in the process. It was time to deploy the holographic cloak. Pulling up a list of Verdissian spaceships, he discovered that most models looked exactly like flying saucers but one or two retained the traditional form of an aeroplane. Snipper selected one of the latter and switched on the holographic projector. Now anyone looking up at him would believe they were seeing a Verdissian spacecraft.

With twenty minutes to go before he would have to land, Snipper finally allowed himself a really good look out of the window. Now he caught his first real glimpse of the Verdissian landscape. It took his breath away. Below a swirling mist of clouds lay rolling hills covered by patchy forest and intersected by rivers and lakes. For a planet bathed in constant daylight for 112 Earth days, it was extraordinarily green. But there was one thing that really bothered him: there was not a single building anywhere in sight.

Snipper frowned. Had he got the wrong co-ordinates? Was the compound where they were keeping Despina miles away on the other side of the planet? He hastily compared his current location with the co-ordinates Cyanne had given him. According to his information, he was only 51 miles from the landing strip. He just hoped to goodness it was true - for it was far too late to change course now.

On reaching an altitude of 60,000 feet, Snipper switched controls to manual and prepared for landing. Gliding downwards at just over 2,000 miles per hour, he banked the lander and then reversed the roll to lose some more speed while maintaining his direction. By 5,000 feet, he was flying at 450 miles per hour - still too fast to land safely. The runway was now less than a mile away and clearly visible - a large clearing in the trees. To one side stood a tall circular building - presumably the space traffic control tower. The hope that the spacelander's holographic cloak was functioning properly flitted briefly through Snipper's mind. But the thought was quickly forgotten as he focussed on getting the plane down safely. He swept his wings forward, lowered his landing gear and was just about to bank again when a voice suddenly came through the intercom.

Pilot, please reduce your speed immediately. This is the space traffic control tower. Landings are not permitted at speeds of over 150 distons per lapss.

For a moment, Snipper almost panicked - put off stride by the unnecessary and distracting warning. He was perfectly well aware that he was going too fast. He just needed a little peace and quiet to focus. Banking the plane just a fraction to the right, he swung away from the landing strip. Then, reversing the roll, he was back on course. At last he had got his speed down to an acceptable 240 miles per hour. By now he was just 200 feet above the runway and seconds from landing.

Easing the nose forwards, Snipper felt the wheels touch down and immediately applied the speedbrake. As he was thrown forward against his seat belt, it seemed to him that he was still going at a terrific speed; and the end of the runway appeared alarmingly close. He half expected to hear another warning over the intercom, telling him to slow down. But he *was* slowing down and he did come to a halt, with fifty yards to spare. He could hardly believe it: he had made it - without any damage either to himself or to the spacelander.

Welcome to Verdis, Spaceport 42, said the voice over the intercom. *We hope you had a pleasant flight. Please park your spacecraft in Bay 723 and report to the Reception Desk.*

Following the markings on the runway, Snipper took the spacelander round to his allotted bay and powered down. Then he changed into his Verdissian robes, collected his backpack from the locker and double-checked its contents. Everything seemed to be in order. So he opened the hatch and lowered the stairway.

Stepping out, he was hit by a wall of hot and humid air, only made bearable by a strong breeze. The spaceport was smaller than he had expected and surrounded by low forest. Only two buildings were visible - the control tower he had spotted from the air and a much lower reception building alongside it. Both were circular and not dissimilar to the flying saucers parked near Snipper's spacelander. In front of the reception building were two green hedgehogs dressed in long robes and deep in conversation. Otherwise, the place was deserted - perhaps not surprisingly, for it seemed to be in the middle of nowhere. There were no roads or paths out of the place. Yet the forest itself looked young. Its floor was carpeted with fresh, bright flowers - the air heavy with their scent. And the trees were spindly and short, as though they had just sprung up over the course of a Verdissian day – or a few months, in Earthly terms.

As he made his way down the steps, Snipper thought his backpack seemed surprisingly light. Glancing at his *ubikwe*, he discovered that gravity on Verdis was 10% weaker than on Earth. He paused on the last step, trying to take it all in. Then finally he set foot on this strange, alien planet. It was one small step, but a giant leap into the unknown. Yet the knowledge that he was following in Despina's footsteps was oddly reassuring. Up until this moment he had thought only of how afraid she must be; but now he remembered she was strong and resourceful too.

Striding purposefully across the runway, Snipper headed for the reception building. As he passed the two green hedgehogs chatting near the entrance, he feared they would see through his disguise; he bristled in expectation of a challenge, but there was none. So he continued up the stairs, with only a brief glance back at the spacelander; he was pleased to see it was indistinguishable from a genuine Verdissian spacecraft nearby.

106

Inside the reception building there was not a soul to be seen. Instead, Snipper found himself being addressed by the same disembodied voice as before.

Welcome, said the voice. *Please present your pass and your paw to the scanner.*

Snipper hesitated. He wondered if the scanner would be able to tell the difference between an Earthling's and a Verdissian's pawprint. Yet Woad had been confident enough. His contact had supplied the Cerulean landing party with their passes; he must have also added their details to the necessary systems. On the other hand, Snipper and Cyanne had only been admitted to the landing party at the last moment. Had there been time to add their details, too?

Please try again, said the voice, as a warning light began to flash intermittently. *All pilots, crew and passengers arriving from interplanetary space are required to identify themselves. Failure to comply is a violation of Regulation 76.*

Snipper hastily presented his paw and his pass to the scanner. To his relief, the flashing stopped.

Identification verified, said the voice. *Thank you for using Spaceport 42. We wish you a pleasant onward journey.*

Snipper now followed the signs for the public shuttle service. A lift took him below ground, where he found himself in a hexagonal room with six tunnels running off it. A voice asked Snipper for his destination. He gave the co-ordinates for Despina's compound, and a minute later a small two-hedgehog shuttle appeared from one of the tunnels. Snipper boarded the shuttle, pulled the glass cover over his head and strapped himself in. Then, with the click of his seat belt, he was off.

Snipper prepared himself for a long ride. There had, after all, been no signs of habitation anywhere near the spaceport. But, just a few minutes later, the shuttle emerged into another hexagonal room and announced that he had reached his destination. Disembarking, he took a lift up to ground level and walked out into the middle of a busy Verdissian town square, where every building resembled a flying saucer. He began to wonder whether the Verdissians were not a little obsessed by space travel. But this was no place to stop and gawp. The square was bristling with green hedgehogs, all going about their business, and it was vital that he blend in.

Following the instructions on his *ubikwe*, Snipper made his way across the square, turned left down a side street and then left again.

Here, just yards away on his right, he saw it - the place where the Verdissians were holding Despina. The red double-decker flying saucer was unmistakable. Snipper's heart skipped a beat. For, looking out through the upper window was Despina herself. He had to stop himself from calling out her name. Instead he took a deep breath and prepared himself to play the most challenging part of his life. For he was no longer the Earthling Snipper but Commander Leafy, a senior officer in the Verdissian intelligence corps. Marching up to the front gate, he saluted the two guards in the traditional Verdissian manner.

"May I ask your business, sir?" asked one.

"I've a warrant for the Earthling's transfer," said Snipper, producing the necessary document.

"This doesn't say where she's to be transferred to," said the guard, examining the warrant.

"That's classified," said Snipper a little severely.

"Yes, sir. Sorry, sir."

The guard passed the warrant back to Snipper and opened the gate for him. So far, it all seemed too easy, which only made him feel more nervous. Crossing the lawn, he had to resist the temptation to break into a run. Even the front door was open and unguarded. He went straight in and up the stairs, and there she was - in Verdissian clothes, reading a Verdissian book, but unmistakably Despina.

Despina did not hear Snipper come in, for she was totally absorbed by her book. Unlike the Ceruleans, the Verdissians had encouraged their Earthling companion to learn their language. Indeed, as soon as they were convinced of her innocence, they tried to persuade her to settle down - to create a new life for herself alongside her Verdissian neighbours. But her only wish was to go home. So the guards had remained. Though they did not believe she was capable of escaping back to Earth, there was no telling what she might do in the attempt. It seemed the only books she was ever interested in were those on space navigation and the principles of wormhole stabilization. But, without Snipper's access to simulators or his experience of flying Earthling aircraft, she was never able to progress from theory to practice.

"Despina," said Snipper gently.

She turned round slowly - wearily. Someone had said her name, and the voice seemed so familiar and so dear to her. Yet she knew it could not be her friend.

"Despina, it's me," said Snipper.

As she looked at him, with his green face and Verdissian robes - looking so like her friend and yet clearly not her friend, she felt she must be going mad. She turned away, holding back the tears by sheer force of will.

"Who are you? What do you want?" she asked in a strained voice.

"Don't you recognize me? It's Snipper. I've come to take you home."

109

Despina turned round again. This time she was crying - but they were tears of happiness. She leapt up from her seat, and the two hedgehogs hugged each other tightly - almost afraid to let go.

"I don't... How did you...?" murmured Despina.

"There's no time to explain," said Snipper. "All you need to know for now is I'm Commander Leafy and I'm here to transfer you to another facility."

Despina nodded and, wiping away the tears, followed Snipper to the head of the stairs.

"Excuse me, sir!" It was Peridot, who had suddenly appeared. "What are you doing?"

"I'm transferring the prisoner to another facility," said Snipper, with all the authority he could muster.

"Prisoner?" repeated Peridot.

"Yes, the Earthling, Despina."

"But Despina's our guest, sir - not a prisoner."

"Aren't I?" asked Despina defiantly. "What are the guards for then? If I'm free, I want to go home."

"Despina, we've been through this before. You know why you can't go home. And, as soon as we're satisfied you've truly accepted your new life here on Verdis, there'll be no further need for guards. Sir," she said, turning to Snipper, "I'd like to see your warrant, please."

Snipper produced the warrant, and Peridot examined it carefully. No one had told her Despina was to move. And who was this Commander Leafy anyway? She had never heard of him. Yet the warrant seemed perfectly genuine. She returned the document to Snipper. But, as she did so, she noticed he was beginning to look a little off colour.

"Sir, you're... You're an Earthling!" she exclaimed.

Snipper looked at his paws and was horrified to see the colour was already beginning to wear off. When he looked up again, Peridot was pointing a laser gun at them.

"Put your paws where I can see them! Both of you!"

The two Earthlings raised their paws.

"Despina, who is this hedgehog? Do you know him?"

Despina was silent.

"She knows me. My name's Snipper. I'm a friend and I've come to take her home."

"That, I'm afraid, is out of the question," said Peridot. "Verdis is Despina's home now. And yours too, now you've followed her here. You both know too much. The question is - how did you get here? You can't be a stowaway - these transfer papers are the real thing. You must have had help."

"A moment ago, you described Despina as your guest," said Snipper, ignoring Peridot's question. "It's a funny sort of guest who has to be kidnapped, held at gunpoint and told they may never go home."

111

Peridot looked embarrassed. "We never meant Despina any harm. It was a misunderstanding - one which we regret deeply. But what's done is done. We can't let you go back - either of you. If we did, *we* would be unable to return. The secret of our existence would be out; our mission to study Earth and its inhabitants would be compromised."

"Despina and I are pretty good at keeping secrets," said Snipper, "if we think they're worth keeping. So why would your mission be compromised? And why is your return to Earth so much more important than our own?"

"It's important because our mission is unique. You must surely see," she said excitedly, "that the chance to study another world in the early stages of development - not altogether unlike our own a few centuries ago... Well, it's almost like possessing a time machine. But, for the study to be valid, our work must remain unobserved. Furthermore, if our presence became known, Earthlings everywhere would soon be hunting for aliens. Eventually, we'd be forced to go public. And that really would be the end of our mission. It would also be a disaster for Earth itself. The natural flow of Earthling evolution would be interrupted. Instead of working things out for yourselves, you'd become dependent upon *our* achievements, and Earth would never be the same again. So, you see, it really is in Earth's own interest that our existence be kept secret."

"If that's your concern," said Snipper. "You're already too late. Your existence isn't yet public knowledge, but it *is* known - to the International Space Agency, for one. Your existence and that of the Ceruleans. Commander Woad of the Cerulean Space Force saw to that."

"So the Ceruleans are behind this!" exclaimed Peridot. "And you're working with them!" She now gripped the laser gun in both paws.

"No, you misunderstand me," said Snipper hastily. "The Ceruleans tricked me - just as they tricked you into leaving Earth."

"I don't believe you. Who else could have provided you with your disguise but the Ceruleans? Who else could have got you the warrant for - but no, that has to have been someone on the inside - a Verdissian." Peridot frowned - only a Verdissian who had visited Earth could have met and helped Snipper. It was an unwelcome thought - for that meant Minty, Moss or Kloraphyll, who were not just colleagues but friends. ...Perhaps Kloraphyll had *meant* to disappear, after all. "Who is it?" she demanded anxiously. "Who's the Verdissian traitor?"

"The informer's name is Major Grass," said Snipper.

112

"You're lying," said Peridot angrily. "Major Grass has never visited Earth. So how could he have brought you here?"

"He didn't. Grass is Woad's informer, not mine. It was Woad who visited Earth and brought me here - though under false pretences. Despina, you met him - though you won't know it. He went by the name of Count de Poynte."

"So Peridot and I were right about him!" said Despina. Relaxing a little, she now lowered her paws. And, as there was no challenge from Peridot, Snipper followed suit. "Listen, Snipper, " continued Despina. "You remember Count de Poynte was standing in for Frau Klanger at the Palace Museum, because she was ill? Well, Frau Klanger's a Verdissian - her real name's Lieutenant Kloraphyll. We think de Poynte poisoned her, so he could become music director in her place."

"You're saying he murdered her?" asked Snipper, who was shocked but not altogether surprised.

"Or attempted to – for we never found her," said Peridot, who still clung to the hope that her friend might be alive. Snipper noticed her relaxing her grip on the laser gun, though she did not put it down.

"His motive," explained Despina, "was to get me to play that piece of music by Niemandt. You know that music which I said had a strange unearthly quality about it? That was the Verdissians' emergency evacuation code. We assume he wanted the Verdissians out of the way for some reason."

"You're right, he did," said Snipper. "But, you know, it was never Woad's intention that the Verdissians take you with them. So," he added, turning to Peridot, "why did you?"

"Because our evacuation code was meant to be secret," said Peridot, "like our presence on Earth. What's more, our normal method of communicating was via a network of digital laser devices - not through a performance at a public concert. So, when we heard Despina and her fellow Earthlings playing our secret code, we were worried *and* puzzled. We left the concert immediately and went off to find Kloraphyll. You see, we'd no idea she was off sick - "

"So, it *was* you," interjected Snipper. "You were the hedgehogs Pawline saw leaving the concert early."

Peridot shrugged her shoulders - she had never heard of Pawline. "Kloraphyll," she continued, "was nowhere to be found, but we came across a couple of notes - one of them signed by her and in her writing - or, at least, so we thought, though they were fakes. They persuaded us that Kloraphyll had confided in Despina and there was a real

113

emergency requiring us to leave Earth at once. So we found Despina and asked her where Kloraphyll was. When she denied even knowing her, we thought we'd been betrayed and had to get out quickly. So we abandoned our search for our colleague, took Despina and left. Now we know the truth, we shall go back. Though it may be too late to save Kloraphyll, we shan't rest until we find her... But, of course, none of this explains why the Ceruleans wanted us out of the way - or your own dealings with them, Snipper."

"Well, as I said, it was never part of Woad's plan for Despina to be kidnapped. But she was and I turned up looking for her, so he grabbed his opportunity. He told me Despina had been taken by Verdissian slave traders and promised to help me get her back; but secretly he intended to murder her. When I found out, I jumped ship. As for the Ceruleans' motives... Well, it seems they've found themselves a new home - Earth. And they're not coming in peace. That's why they wanted you out of the way."

Despina stared at Snipper in horrified silence.

"So they're moving to *your* planet!" exclaimed Peridot. "That explains why they refused our offer."

"What offer?" asked Snipper.

"We said they could have a home here on Verdis. Their planet won't be able to support life for much longer, but we've got plenty of room. At first, they accepted - a little grudgingly, perhaps, almost as though they were the ones doing us a favour. Then a few months ago the Cerulean High Command suddenly changed their minds. No explanation was given - not even to their own population. It caused a great deal of unhappiness among the Ceruleans who were in the know. Soon afterwards some of them even defected to us - came over to us with two of their spacelanders and their entire crews. They've been living here on Verdis ever since. But what I still don't understand is how the Ceruleans ever reached Earth. They don't have the technology for interstellar travel."

"If you're talking about wormhole travel," said Snipper, "they claim *they* invented it and *you* stole the secret from them. As for your having offered them a home on Verdis, that seems very odd. They've gone to an awful lot of trouble to prepare for their conquest of Earth. Why would they do that, when they could so easily have had a home here? Is there something wrong with your planet?"

"No, nothing!" protested Peridot, bristling at Snipper's rude question. "But I suppose," she added a little awkwardly, "it's not quite as idyllic as Earth."

"You mean the long days?" asked Snipper.

"Yes - or rather the long nights. A night here lasts 112 Earth days. No one wants to live on the Dark Side, except a few astronomers and meteorologists. And it isn't only the lack of sunlight. It's extremely cold – much of the ground is frozen solid. So we Verdissians live a nomadic lifestyle. You'll have noticed our homes look like spaceships. Well, that's because they *are* spaceships. When the sun finally sinks, we all migrate. As for the Light Side, it's pleasant enough - as you can see. Thick clouds and strong winds prevent the temperature from climbing too high. But we seldom enjoy the clear blue skies and gentle summer breezes we experienced in Hedgermany... There's no point trying to deny it, Earth has a much better climate than Verdis. And, of course, compared to Cerulea, it's a paradise."

"But I still don't understand what any of this has got to do with me," said Despina. "Why would Woad want to kill me? And why wait till now? He had plenty of opportunities back on Earth."

"Back then his intention was simply to use you, not kill you," said Snipper. "It was only after your unexpected abduction - followed, I'm afraid, by me turning up to look for you, that a new idea occurred to him. He thought that, if he could convince us Earthlings we were under threat from the Verdissians, we'd willingly place ourselves under Cerulean protection. So he decided to murder you and pin it on the Verdissians. Your lifeless body was to provide the physical proof of the Verdissian threat; I was to be the witness. And this, he believed, would pave the way for the Ceruleans to take over our planet. It sounds crazy, I know, but they actually believed we wouldn't mind being ruled by them - because of their natural superiority!"

"I can believe that easily enough," said Peridot wryly. "They're blinded by arrogance. They hate us Verdissians partly because they're jealous of our technology but also because they despise our practice of democracy. Cerulea's a single country, ruled by a few unelected hedgehogs, whereas Verdis is made up of many nations, each electing its own government. According to the Ceruleans, our system makes us weak. As for Earth, they're bound to consider you as not only weak but inferior, too. Though, in my opinion, you're ahead of the Ceruleans in so many ways. Your belief that all hedgehogs are created equal, your love of liberty - "

"Talking of our love of liberty," interrupted Despina, "perhaps now you'll let us go. You must surely see your policy of non-interference has failed - and that we *must* go back to warn our fellow Earthlings of the Cerulean threat."

Peridot nodded and finally laid down her laser gun. "I'll speak to my colleagues. But it may take a while to get official agreement for your release, and you're in a hurry, so I don't suggest you wait. I'll smuggle you out. There'll be time enough for explanations after you've gone. But, Snipper, you know you won't get as far as the front gate if you look like that."

"That's all right. I've brought supplies with me." So saying, he pulled out a bottle of *viritinctus*, took a swig at it and then passed it to Despina. "It'll be easier at the spaceport," he explained, "if you're green, as well. There's plenty for both of us. What I don't have is anything to turn us blue."

"You mean we're not going home after all?" asked Despina; she was unable to hide her disappointment.

"Not yet," said Snipper. "I'm afraid our first port of call must be Cerulea. Warning Earth isn't enough. We have to try and stop the Ceruleans from coming at all."

"How will you do that?" asked Peridot. She could see Despina's friend was an extraordinary hedgehog. Somehow, he had learnt to speak Verdissian and land a spacecraft; he had also got the better of Woad and his crew. But even he could not defeat the entire Cerulean population on his own. Perhaps the Verdissian authorities could be persuaded to help, but it would take time and there was precious little of that. So she kept her thoughts to herself. She had no wish to make promises she could not keep.

"Well," said Snipper, thinking out loud, "Our best form of defence would be to keep them out of our solar system altogether. So, if we could destroy the ISVs' wormhole capability, that would do it..."

"What's an ISV?" asked Despina.

"An interstellar space vehicle - a large Cerulean spaceship designed to travel through wormholes."

"So that's how you got here? On one of their ISVs?"

"No, that's how I got to this solar system, but you can't land an ISV. The Ceruleans have a smaller craft for that – spacelanders: they're halfway between a rocket and an aeroplane but *not* equipped with wormhole technology. So I stole one of those."

"You mean you just helped yourself to a spacelander and flew to Verdis?" asked Peridot. "The Ceruleans didn't bother to pursue you?"

"Well, I had a little help from a sympathetic Cerulean," said Snipper. "I also slipped away while the crew were sleeping, so I'd be well within Verdissian airspace by the time they could respond to the alarm. In any case, there would have been no point in pursuing me. It was obvious I was onto them, so I wasn't going to believe *you'd* murdered Despina. Though I imagine they'd like to have their spacelander back..."

"Not enough to invade our airspace," said Peridot. "The spacelanders are small and much cheaper to build than an ISV. They've got dozens of them. One fewer won't make much difference."

"So how are we going to destroy their wormhole stabilizers?" asked Despina, returning to the point. "I mean, we can't just board their ISVs one by one."

"To be honest, I've no idea how we can do it," said Snipper, bleakly. "We may have to play it by ear once we get there - or else come up with a different plan altogether."

"No, I think you're on the right track," said Peridot. "The key point is that, while the Ceruleans may have stolen our wormhole technology, I doubt very much they understand the science behind it. It's complicated stuff - it's rocket science. To be honest, I don't really get it, myself - I'm a doctor, not a physicist. But you don't need to understand it to use it. All the Ceruleans had to do was steal the computer code for making wormhole stabilizers. They then feed that into their onboard 3D printers, press print and out comes a stabilizer. It's nice and easy. But that means, if they lose the code, they won't know how to rebuild it."

"But surely," said Despina, "if we're talking about a computer code, they'll have copies."

"In any case," added Snipper, "they've already printed off their stabilizers - they're using them."

"True," agreed Peridot, "but each wormhole stabilizer can only be used once. You see, if a stabilizer picks up any impurities, it becomes unreliable, and you really don't want that. It's only the negative energy generated by the stabilizer which stops the wormhole collapsing - and destroying everything and everyone inside it. So we always print off a fresh one for every new wormhole."

"But what about the copies they'll have made?" persisted Despina. "Are you suggesting we hack into the onboard computer systems of every ISV?"

"I don't think that'll be necessary," said Peridot. "You see, there's a weakness in their system. Every time one of their spaceships enters Cerulean airspace, it has to connect with Mission Control to pick up fresh orders and download any patches or upgrades. So, if you can corrupt the code at source, you can corrupt it on all the ISVs, too."

"But how often are the ISVs in Cerulean airspace?" asked Despina. "They must be dispersed all over the universe."

"Not if they're planning an invasion," said Snipper. "The fleet will assemble for that. So, if we can get into their Mission Control Centre, this might actually work. Any ideas, Peridot, how we might get in?"

"Certainly. In fact, I can even give you the co-ordinates and a plan of the interior. I can also get you pass keys, uniforms, space suits and a Cerulean hover-bike. You see, we did rather well out of those Cerulean defectors when they came over to us. And it won't take me long to mix up some *cerutinctus* to turn you both blue."

"Great!" said Snipper. "That just leaves the question of transport. The spacelander will get us to Cerulea but, as you know, it won't get us home."

"You'd better come back here," said Peridot. "I'll give you a lift home in Rusty. That's my two-hedgehog spacevessel, which I'm pretty sure could take three at a squeeze. It's just a matter of rigging up a third seat. Rusty's small but fast and, most importantly, wormhole-enabled."

"I thought only a really big spacecraft could navigate a wormhole," said Snipper.

"If you're talking about Cerulean technology, yes. But we Verdissians are still a little ahead, despite all their thieving."

"I see," said Snipper, thoughtfully. "Look, I don't suppose we could just borrow Rusty, could we? It would give us a lot more flexibility."

Peridot looked shocked. She was pretty sure that 'borrow' was an Earthling euphemism for 'take and never bring back'. But then the seriousness of the situation seemed to win her over. "Well, all right then - if you think you know what you're doing. I take it you *do* know how to identify, stabilize and expand a wormhole?"

Snipper nodded.

"In that case," continued Peridot, "you'd better take my key fob. You'll need to go to Spaceport 42, bay 716. There's a manual in the pocket under the dashboard. But Cerulean and Verdissian spacecraft work in broadly the same manner. Hardly surprising, I suppose, given they stole the technology from us. All the same, you'll find my spacevessel's a lot easier to handle than a Cerulean spaceship - a lot more intuitive. Oh, and one more thing - Rusty's got an invisibility shield. Only the very latest Verdissian models have that. I think you'll find it's a big improvement on the holographic cloak."

Chapter Eleven

Back at the spaceport, Snipper was struck by just how small Rusty was compared to his Cerulean spacelander - let alone an ISV; he was surprised the machine was robust enough to stand up to the rigours of wormhole travel.

Inside, they found a neat pile of towels, sleeping bag liners, Cerulean uniforms and space suits, and the clothes Despina had been wearing at the concert. The food cupboard was stocked with supplies enough to feed an army. It also contained some bottles of *cerutinctus*, toothbrushes, pass keys, a tiny data file and a note from Peridot, wishing them good luck. As promised, the manual was under the dashboard. Snipper read the section devoted to lift-off but decided the rest could wait. Then he switched on the microphone.

"Preparing for lift-off," he announced in Verdissian. "Please give the all-clear."

"All-clear granted," came the reply. *"Lift-off is in 10 seconds and counting... 3, 2, 1..."*

Snipper pulled a lever, and the tiny spacevessel sprang up into the sky, pushing the two hedgehogs down into their seats; but the ascent was a great deal gentler than it had been in a spacelander. Watching the altimeter, Snipper noticed they were climbing really quite slowly.

Then, as the pressure began to fall away, he nudged Rusty into an orbital path. Shortly afterwards, a small doll on a piece of string floated gently upwards into the glass dome. Snipper noticed it was an Earthling doll - a souvenir from Peridot's stay in Hedgermany.

"Are you all right, Despina?" he asked.

"I'm fine. I was expecting the launch to be a lot more uncomfortable than that. No doubt I should put the smooth ascent down to your expert piloting!"

"Of course you should!" said Snipper, laughing. He was glad to see Despina had not lost her sense of humour after all she had been through. "But you know I wasn't just talking about the take-off."

"Well, I'm not sorry to be leaving," said Despina. "Not that they ever laid a paw on me, but I can't tell you how lonely I was. I'm just glad it's all over now."

"Except, of course, it isn't," said Snipper guiltily. "You may come to wish I'd left you in peace on Verdis. You do know we may never...?"

"You don't need to tell me," said Despina. "I know our chances of making it back to Earth are slim. Yet somehow, now we're together, I feel as though everything's going to turn out all right."

"Yes, I know what you mean," said Snipper, "I feel the same."

"Oh look!" said Despina suddenly. "Look down there!"

Snipper looked. It was twilight on Verdis directly below them. The cloud cover was as thick as ever but, above the clouds, a fleet of Verdissian mobile homes was making its way back to the Light Side. The patch of land they were leaving would not see daylight again for another 112 Earth days. It was an extraordinary sight - hundreds of flying saucers of every shape and size, and here and there a few old-fashioned spacecraft similar to the Cerulean spacelanders.

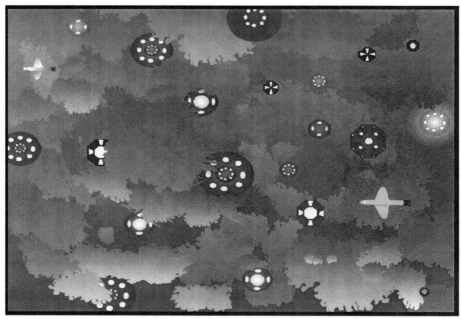

But, passing over the Verdissian migration at orbital velocity, the two Earthlings soon found themselves alone once more. Before long, they were flying over the Dark Side. Rain clouds now turned to snow. Then, as the sky gradually cleared, an immense white wilderness came into view, bathed in the light of three moons. Though they covered thousands of miles, they did not see a single sign of habitation. It was as though an arctic winter covered half the planet.

Eventually, a pale blue disc came into view. It was smaller but more colourful than the Verdissian moons. Snipper pulled a lever, propelling Rusty out of orbit. Then he activated the invisibility shield and set a straight course for Cerulea.

"It looks quite close," said Despina, "How long do you think it will take us to get there?"

"Twenty-two and half Cerulean hours," said Snipper, reading the spacenav on his dashboard. "That's just over thirty hours in Earth time.

So we may as well make ourselves comfortable and switch on the gravity-simulator."

"Hmm, I wonder how that works in a tiny spaceboat like this," said Despina. "If it's going to spin, we'll end up standing on the dashboard. Everything's the wrong way up!"

"There's one way to find out," said Snipper, with his nose back in the manual. "According to the instructions, I just have to press this button here."

So saying, he pressed the button. A yellow light began to flash and, a moment later, their seatbelts sprang open. As the two hedgehogs floated away, the seats collapsed into the floor, almost as though someone had stuck a pin in them, and up popped two dining chairs and a small table. Next thing they knew, the floor had swivelled 90° and the yellow light had turned blue. Snipper motioned to Despina. The two hedgehogs grabbed hold of a rail, just as the spacevessel began to spin. Then, as the spinning got faster and faster, the stars seemed to shoot across the sky and their feet gradually descended, until eventually they were standing quite firmly on the floor. The acceleration now stopped, and the sensation of spinning disappeared with it.

As soon as this was all over, Snipper and Despina set about examining the contents of their food cupboard, for they were both very hungry. Before long they were tucking into a hearty meal, washed down with a strong dose of *cerutinctus.* Chatting away for an hour or so, they gradually filled each other in on everything that had occurred over the last few months. When they were done, Snipper brought out his holographic device so they could get a feel for Cerulea's geography. Gently spinning the pale blue holographic globe, he located the Cerulean Space Fleet's Mission Control Centre. Then he tapped the spot, and the globe disappeared to be replaced by a floorplan. The two hedgehogs had a good look at this, worked out their route and then decided to get some rest.

Snipper put away the holographic device and got out the operating manual from under the dashboard. Pawing over it, he quickly discovered that Rusty was equipped with every luxury. As well as a tiny shower cubicle, it had a pull-out basin, where they were able to brush their teeth, and two luxuriously soft sleeping bags. Snipper fixed the bags to the specially provided moorings. Then, when they were ready for bed, he switched off the gravity-sim. The two hedgehogs floated up into their bags and pulled the drawer strings tight.

With the light off, Cerulea and its surrounding stars glowed so brightly Snipper believed he could never tire of such a view. Yet he would gladly give up space travel forever. All he really cared about now was saving his planet and getting Despina home safely.

"Despina," he said softly, "are you awake?"

"Yes," she murmured. "It's so comfortable like this, isn't it? Too comfortable to waste it being asleep. I wonder if I could build some sort of anti-gravity device when we get back home."

Snipper laughed but then became serious again: "Look, if we do make it back to Earth, I think you and I..." His voice tailed away.

"Yes?" queried Despina.

Snipper started again, this time assuming a more casual tone. "I was thinking maybe we should tie the knot. That way, it'll be a lot easier for me to keep an eye on you, next time someone gets it into their head to kidnap you."

There was a brief silence, broken only by the thumping of Snipper's heart.

"Tie the knot? Do you mean...?"

"I mean get married," said Snipper quickly.

"Yes, I suppose that makes sense," said Despina, trying to match his casual tone and hide her true feelings. "Yes, I agree – let's do it."

"Well, good," said Snipper. "I'm glad we've got that settled."

"So am I," said Despina. "Good night, Snipper."

"Good night, Despina. Sleep well."

Chapter Twelve

The next couple of days were happy ones. Snipper and Despina knew their voyage to Cerulea might be a one-way trip. They knew they would be risking their lives and that the future of their planet was at stake. Yet this only made the short time together more precious. Even when they were focussed on preparing for their mission – which was most of the time – they felt strangely happy. During this period, Despina concentrated on teaching herself the Cerulean language. Two days was, of course, not long enough for her to become fluent like Snipper, but the osmotic method was fast. By the time they reached Cerulea, she had acquired a good basic understanding of the language and was able to sing without a trace of an Earthling accent. Snipper, meanwhile, kept an eye on Rusty's controls. He also continued to study the Mission Control floorplan, until he knew the place like the back of his paw.

On the third and final morning of their voyage to Cerulea, Snipper and Despina were woken by the on-board alarm clock. It was just before noon Cerulean local time and the sun was directly overhead. Slipping straight out of their sleeping bags, they switched the gravity-sim back on and made themselves breakfast.

By the time they had finished, cleared away, brushed their teeth and dressed, they were just twenty minutes away from Cerulea's thin atmosphere. Assembled in the middle distance were five vast Cerulean spaceships, one of which Snipper thought he recognized as the *ISV Resurgence*. Fortunately, Rusty was invisible and their presence remained undetected.

With the cabin now returned to landing mode, Snipper and Despina strapped themselves into their seats. Snipper then double-checked the manual. He rather regretted having to land a new model of spacecraft, just when he had been getting used to the spacelander. But he need not have worried. He had only to punch in the landing co-ordinates and then press *Accept*, when asked if he was sure he wanted to land.

At an altitude of 70,000 feet, they entered the Cerulean atmosphere. There were no flames this time and the ride was gentler, for they had managed to slow down to a rather leisurely 3,000 miles per hour. At 28,000 feet, Snipper pressed the *Inflate* button; Rusty expanded like a balloon, slowing them down still further.

While Snipper was busy monitoring their descent on various computer screens, Despina was gazing out of the window. Beneath a thin cover of wispy cloud lay an inhospitable world of ice and snow. There was no sign of life down there - neither animal nor plant. To a casual observer it might not have seemed so very different to the Dark Side on Verdis or the North Pole on Earth. Yet they were now just 40° south of the equator; and Cerulea had no equivalent of the Dark Side - for here a day lasted just twenty-one Earth hours. No wonder the Ceruleans were in such a hurry to leave. But, for all that, there was an eerie beauty about their planet. Its surface was pristine - unmarked by hedgehog paw. The snow glistened and sparkled in the sun. And, as a restless sea crashed against an icy shore, fountains of spray were sent high into the air.

With just 200 feet to go, they were now descending at a very gentle 80 miles per hour. Searching the ground for a good place to land, Snipper spotted a low, flat-bottomed ravine. It was just deep enough to hide Rusty but shallow enough for them to climb out of without the aid of equipment. Engaging the main thruster, he sent Rusty over to the ravine; and, at 100 feet, he lowered the landing gear. Ten seconds later, they touched down, a jet of air cushioning their landing and sending up a flurry of snow.

Snipper pressed *deflate* and turned off the engine. Then he surveyed the snowy ravine. On their left flank, a frozen river wound its way past them towards the open sea - which was just eight miles away

127

according to the onboard spacenav. On their right, was a deep shadow cast by the ravine's edge - which seemed to play tricks on the eyes.

"What was that?" asked Snipper.

"What was what?" responded Despina, who had been looking the other way.

"I thought I saw something move. Yes, there, behind that rock!"

Despina looked but saw nothing. "What do you want to do?"

"We'd better investigate," said Snipper. "Rusty may be invisible but our landing won't have gone unnoticed if there's someone there. All the same, let's keep our cool. We may be able to convince them we're legitimate."

"What about the invisibility shield? Are you going to leave it on?"

Snipper shook his head. "Spacelanders don't have invisibility shields, so they'll already know it's a Verdissian spacecraft. I think it'll look less suspicious if we turn the shield off. I can say we captured Rusty from the Verdissians. Then, if we manage to get rid of whoever it is out there, I'll turn the shield back on again."

"You think they'll believe you?"

"I think we should have our laser guns ready in case they don't."

The two hedgehogs tucked their lasers into their trouser pockets. Then they activated the thermostatic heating systems in their space suits and put on their space helmets. The air outside was -82° C and contained only half the oxygen they were used to on Earth. Without these artificial aids, they would not survive for long.

Climbing out of their spacevessel, they now walked straight over to the rock where Snipper had seen the movement. As they did so, two Cerulean hoglets emerged shyly from their hiding place.

"Please don't tell on us!" said the older of the two.

"What are you doing here?" asked Snipper a little sternly, responding to their cue.

"We're spotting spacecraft," said the younger hoglet.

"But we're not doing any harm!" added the older.

"Hmm," said Snipper. "*We'll* be the judge of that. You'd better show us your notes."

The older hoglet brought out a small holographic device and showed it to Snipper. Alongside a list of numbers were pictures of spacecraft. The design and size varied, but they were all circular, like Verdissian spacecraft. There was even a tiny two-hedgehog spacevessel very similar to Rusty. Others were family-sized and a few looked as though they would take a very large crew.

"You've seen these?" asked Snipper. "Here? All of them?"

"Yes, all of them!" said the hoglet proudly. "Our Dad's a test pilot too, you see. That's how we found out they were building a new kind of circular spacecraft. Is it true they're all wormhole-enabled, like the ones the Verdissians have?"

"So your Dad knows you're here?"

"Oh, no! He'd be furious. We followed him. But you *won't* tell on us, will you?"

"I see," said Snipper thoughtfully. "So what else have you seen?"

"We found the harbour where all the flying saucers go to bed!" piped up the younger hoglet, not wishing to be left out. As he pointed, Snipper made a mental note of the direction.

"You *won't* tell our Dad, will you?" persisted the older hoglet.

Snipper smiled. "No, we won't. But you must promise us something in return."

The two hoglets nodded vigorously.

"You mustn't tell anybody what you saw today. This spacevessel of ours is very special. In fact, it's a Top Secret model, which even the other test pilots aren't allowed to know about."

"No way!" exclaimed the two hoglets together in breathless excitement.

"It's that invisibility thing, isn't it?" added the older one. "That was super cool."

"I'm glad you like it," said Snipper. "Now, I think you'd better both be on your way. Go on! Off with you!"

The hoglets sighed but did not argue. Fetching a hover-bike from behind the rock, they took one last wistful look at Rusty and were gone.

"So their technology's not as far behind the Verdissians' as we thought," said Despina, once the hoglets were out of earshot. "Perhaps they've been stealing again."

"I imagine they have," said Snipper. "But you know what this means, don't you? Stopping the ISVs won't be enough. Once they roll out these new spacevessels, every last household on Cerulea will have its own wormhole-enabled spacecraft."

"Does that matter?" asked Despina. "You said yourself that, after we've fed the corrupt data into their IT systems, it'll be uploaded to the entire fleet."

"To the ISVs, yes, because they belong to the Cerulean Space Force. But I very much doubt any civilians will be hooking up with Mission Control."

"I see," said Despina, frowning. "So we have to destroy the test vessels too. But where do you want to start?"

"Mission Control," said Snipper decisively. "We know the test vessels are kept somewhere to the south of here, but that's all we know. Whereas we've got the exact location for Mission Control." Switching on his holographic device, he conjured up a 3D map supplied by Peridot; a red flashing dot marked their own location. "Here - right next to the spaceport," he said, pointing to an area tagged with Cerulean letters. "What's more, we actually have a plan for dealing with the ISVs."

"True," said Despina, "but I'm pretty sure I do know where the test facility is." As a professional hydrologist, she had quickly cast an expert eye over the sea, rivers and lakes. "Those hoglets said they'd seen the harbour where the test vessels are kept, didn't they? Well, at first I assumed they were talking about a natural sea harbour somewhere along this coast. But the sea looks pretty rough round here. And take a look at this lake: it's the only one that isn't frozen, a canal connects it to the sea, and there's even a dam to control the flow."

"Yes, I see what you mean," said Snipper. "But I wonder why they don't keep the fleet on dry land like the spacelanders."

"It must be for camouflage," said Despina. "The test vessels are meant to be secret, after all."

130

"Yes, but they've got invisibility shields... Actually, no, they don't! The hoglets *saw* all the other spacevessels. And, when I said Rusty was a special model, they assumed I was talking about the invisibility shield. Somehow, that's the one secret the Verdissians have managed to keep to themselves - for now, at least. So you're right, they must be using the lake for camouflage. Do you have any ideas why they've built this canal to the sea? It looks too narrow for transport."

"Well, assuming their seas and lakes are anything like ours, I'd say they've built the canal so they can pump sea water into the lake. Salt water freezes at a lower temperature than fresh. So, by adding salt water to the lake, they prevent it from icing over. And the dam must be to regulate the salt input. They won't want to add any more than is strictly necessary, given how corrosive it is."

The two hedgehogs were now convinced they did know the location of the test facility. But Mission Control remained the first target of their planned attack. It was the closer of the two and would give them a little time to work out a way to wreck the test vessels. But, however they set about it, they both knew that, until they had destroyed the Ceruleans' ability to travel through wormholes, Earth would remain vulnerable. Conscious of this, they unloaded their hover-bike in thoughtful silence, each of them racking their brains for a solution. Snipper was still deep in thought as he attached his backpack to the hover-bike, switched Rusty's invisibility shield back on and locked the door. But now, finally, with him in the driving seat and Despina behind, they were off.

The hover-bike was quiet, smooth and fast, as it swept along on a cushion of air, never once touching the snow. Snipper was tempted to test the machine's limits but it was no time for games. As they emerged from the ravine, they found themselves in a wide, U-shaped valley. The high mountains on either side were blanketed in fresh snow. Frozen waterfalls and rocky summits were the only features in this empty white landscape. Yet it was dazzling, for the waterfalls sparkled in the sunlight, and the rocky summits soared up into an intense Cerulean sky. It reminded Snipper of the Altispine Mountains back on Earth. But the resemblance was an illusion, because the *whole* of Cerulea was covered in ice and snow.

After a few minutes, they came to a cleft in the mountains. Passing through, they found the coast now on their left. There was no beach visible, for an ice sheet spread out from the land over the sea, its advance slowed only by the waves crashing against it. Ahead was a frozen river. Snipper took the hover-bike over the river and turned right up another U-shaped valley, straight past a spaceport parked up with around twenty spacelanders.

"This is it," warned Snipper. "Are you ready?"

Despina looked around. There was little sign of habitation beyond the spaceport - just three igloos and a fleet of hover-bikes. She squeezed Snipper's arm in silent assent. Parking their hover-bike next to the others, they made their way over to the nearest igloo. As they did so, three Ceruleans emerged from it and saluted. The two Earthlings returned the salute in silence, avoiding any eye contact.

They entered the igloo through a low opening and down a short flight of steps. It was surprisingly spacious inside, housing four hedgehog-sized glass pods. Selecting one each, they tapped in a special code, supplied by Peridot's defectors. Then they played a couple of voice samples in which the same defectors gave the command to open.

Descending swiftly and smoothly, the pods took Snipper and Despina deep below ground, where they emerged into a large cloakroom. Most of the lockers were already taken and a long line of boots occupied the racks. Puddles of recently melted snow on the floor and the sound of voices retreating suggested the place was in constant use. Snipper slipped into his pocket the tiny electronic device given him by Peridot and then deposited his backpack in one of the lockers, together with their helmets, boots and space suits. Then, dressed in their Cerulean Space Fleet uniforms, they proceeded out into a long underground passage bristling with Ceruleans. Following Peridot's floorplan, they made their way through the accommodation area, past Mission Control itself and a row of offices. And they had just got as far as the plant room when a bell sounded. A voice over the loud speaker was summoning all space force officers to the conference hall. Suddenly the flow of hedgehogs was going all one way - in the opposite direction to the two Earthlings.

Snipper grabbed Despina's paw and led her into the plant room, a cavernous space devoted entirely to trees and shrubs; lit with redirected sunlight and warmed by heaters, these plants provided the oxygen the Ceruleans needed to survive.

"What's the plan?" asked Despina. "Are we going to hide here until they've all disappeared into their conference?"

"On the contrary. I think we should go with them and find out what it's all about. It must be pretty important if they've summoned the entire officer corps."

"But, Snipper, if the Ceruleans are all in conference together, surely it's the perfect opportunity for us to work undisturbed. Besides, someone might recognize you."

"That's a possibility. But, remember, no one's expecting to see me here and we're both in disguise. I think it's a risk worth taking. They may be about to discuss the invasion plans..."

"All right then," said Despina, without further argument. She could see his point and trusted his judgement.

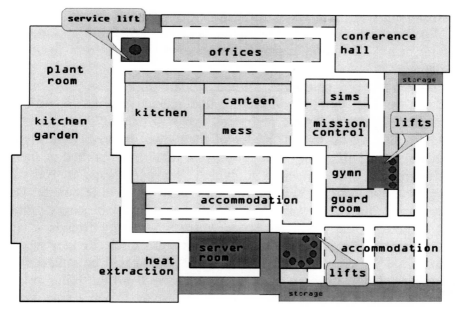

By the time they arrived in the conference hall, it was already crowded, humming with the chatter of hundreds of hedgehogs. On the stage at the front was a hedgehog known to both Snipper and Despina – though until now *she* had only ever seen him in his Earthling disguise, as Count de Poynte.

Arms crossed, Commander Woad surveyed the crowd, waiting impatiently as the last few officers found themselves seats. Then he coughed, and there was immediate silence. Snipper set his *ubikwe* to record mode.

"Gentlehogs," began Woad, "as you know all too well, our beloved planet is dying. We must leave Cerulea and find a new place to live. Some of you will have heard the rumour that we were offered - but refused - a new home on Verdis. And you may have wondered why. A few have even disobeyed orders and travelled to Verdis, taking with them two of our spacelanders. These defectors are a disgrace to their uniform. None of them will ever be allowed to return, on pain of death. And very soon they will learn the full extent of their foolishness. For we have no need of Verdissian charity. We've found another planet, called Earth, which not only supports life but has everything we could hope for. Its air is breathable and its climate healthy. There are forests, open grasslands and rivers teeming with life. And, unlike Verdissian nights, *its* nights are short. So there will be no need for us to adopt the Verdissians' restless nomadic lifestyle."

Woad waved a paw. A holographic projection of Earth appeared in all its beauty, bringing a gasp of wonder and excitement from the audience.

"Furthermore," continued Woad, "the population of brown hedgehogs who currently dominate the planet pose no significant obstacle. They're backward and weak and will benefit from our rule. As it is, they've no overall leader of their own. Instead, they divide themselves into what they call countries - some two hundred of them, each with its own government, which is sheer chaos as you can imagine - and another reason why they need us to take charge. But they won't have to wait long. For, in thirty-two hours' time, contingents of the Cerulean Space Force - you, my friends - will simultaneously land at every rocket and missile launch site they've got. Meanwhile the crew of their orbital space station will be replaced by Ceruleans. This will serve as an important lesson. An Earthling's place is on his planet serving us - not exploring space. Soon - very soon, control of the skies and space around Earth will rest entirely in Cerulean paws. Any questions?"

"Sir!" said an enthusiastic young officer at the front. "Do you think there'll be resistance?"

"Yes. But our spacelanders will be disguised as Earthling vessels - civilian aeroplanes in distress, which have been forced to make an emergency landing. Only as we emerge from our spacecraft will they learn who we really are. And by then it will be too late for them. Any resistance will be futile. But, if they *are* foolish enough to fight - and I fear they are, we must crush them without mercy."

"Sir, is it true there's an Earthling by the name of Snipper, who already knows we're coming?"

"There *was* such an Earthling and, for a short while, he was something of a thorn in our side. But you can rest assured he no longer poses any threat to our plans whatsoever."

"But, sir, won't he warn the other Earthlings?"

"No, for by now he is certainly dead. Like the fool he was, he stole one of our spacelanders in an attempt to land on Verdis. But no Earthling is capable of landing such a sophisticated machine. He'll either have burnt up as he entered the Verdissian atmosphere or else have bounced off into deep space, without enough fuel ever to return."

"But, sir, how do we - "

Woad put up his paw, commanding silence. "Enough questions. For I now have the honour to pass you over to Space Marshall Indigo, our illustrious commander-in-chief."

Indigo walked up onto the stage to wild applause. When this had died down, he briefed his officers on their various duties. Snipper listened carefully, taking in as much as he could; but the briefing lasted over an hour, and he was relieved he had recorded it on his *ubikwe*. Finally, Indigo wished his officers well and told them to pack their bags. They were to report for duty in twelve hours – twenty-one hours in Earth-time. As they began to pile out of the conference hall, Snipper and Despina moved with the flow. Inching their way towards the exit, Snipper suddenly caught sight of Cyanne and Flight Lieutenant Azziur. They were both looking his way and would no doubt have caught his eye, had he been less experienced at operating under cover; but he looked away without showing even a flicker of recognition.

Out in the corridor, Snipper and Despina walked away as fast as they dared, back past the plant room. They turned left, left again and right until they reached the server room. Then, using the password provided by Peridot, they let themselves in, closing the door swiftly behind them. The room was thankfully unoccupied, and they were now free to speak.

"What exactly was Woad saying about the international space station?" asked Despina. Her imperfect grasp of the Cerulean language made her wonder if she had heard right.

"He's going to replace the crew with Ceruleans," said Snipper grimly.

"So Pawline and Schnüffel..."

"Yes, I know. But all we can do for them now is to get a move on and destroy that wormhole code. You'd better stand guard while I run a search."

Taking a seat at the IT administrator's desk, Snipper logged on. He told the system to look for any files containing the words *wormhole stabilizer*. Then he waited. Seconds passed and then minutes.

"How's it going?" asked Despina anxiously.

"I don't know. There seem to be an awful lot of - No, wait! There it is!" Snipper immediately inserted the tiny electronic device provided by Peridot and pasted her false code over the Ceruleans' clean version, including all their back-up files. Then, as quickly as he could, he pocketed the device, shut down the computer and joined Despina at the door.

"Any sign of activity out there?" he whispered.

"None at all."

Snipper opened the door a crack. The coast was clear. The two hedgehogs slipped out and locked the door behind them. Then they made their way back towards the lifts. Luckily, there were very few hedgehogs about now. Snipper guessed they were all busy packing and saying goodbye to their families.

"Snipper!" exclaimed a voice behind them. "It really *is* you, isn't it?"

They carried on walking.

"Snipper, stop, it's me - Cyanne!"

Snipper turned round. It was indeed Cyanne, and she was beckoning to them. They said nothing but followed her into what was clearly her private room.

"Hello, Cyanne," said Snipper with a smile, as they closed the door behind them. "This is my friend, Despina."

"Pleased to meet you," said Cyanne, with genuine but brisk pleasure. "And I'm very glad to see you made it, Snipper. But, I must warn you, you've already been recognized. Azziur saw you at the briefing. I tried to persuade him it couldn't have been you and I may have bought you some time. He's gone to check the CCTV. There's no coverage here in the accommodation block, but the cameras will have caught you on the way in. And, once he's confirmed his suspicions, he'll go straight to Commander Woad. But you must have known you were taking a huge risk coming here. So why *did* you come?"

"To save Earth from a Cerulean invasion," said Snipper grimly.

139

"Then I'm afraid you're too late. You heard what they said in the briefing - the entire Cerulean Space Force is already getting ready to leave for Earth. I'm sorry - but that's the way it is."

"Maybe," said Snipper, "but we have to try." He made a move towards the door.

"What exactly do you have in mind?" asked Cyanne suspiciously.

Snipper saw her glance at her laser gun, which was lying on the bedside table. He knew that, though she had risked her life to help him save Despina, there were limits to what she would be prepared to do for him. Her first loyalty would still be to her own kind. And the Ceruleans needed somewhere to live.

"Did you know about the Verdissians' offer of a new home?" he asked, not knowing whether he would get an honest answer.

"No, I didn't. And - before you say anything - yes, we were wrong to refuse. But what's done is done. We can't expect the Verdissians to renew their offer, so Earth is still our only hope. And, to be frank, if I really thought you could stop the invasion, I'd hand you in right now myself. I may have helped you before, but that was different. Surely even you must understand that - or do you expect us to just sit here and wait to die?"

"Of course I don't - but it's not just about a new home, is it? This is to be a conquest - Woad made that very clear - as did you when we discussed this before."

"So what *were* you planning to do?" asked Cyanne, ignoring his last comment. "I assume the Verdissians are in on this - seeing how good your disguises are."

"Yes, we had a little help. As for our plans, well..." Snipper hesitated. He did not want to give Cyanne more information than necessary. But, if he refused to tell her anything at all, that would only make her more suspicious. "We were going to corrupt the computer code for your wormhole stabilizers," he said at last. He hoped that, by implying their plan was yet to be carried out, she would be lulled into a false sense of security. The sabotage could not, in any case, be undone. And he naturally made no mention of the test fleet.

"An interesting idea," said Cyanne, "but I'm afraid I shall have to disappoint you." She grabbed her laser gun and pointed it at the two Earthlings. "Listen, I don't want either of you to get hurt, so I'm going to give you a head start. You've got ten Earth-minutes. Then I shall go to Commander Woad myself - if Azziur hasn't already done so. I urge you to use those ten minutes to get away and save yourselves while you can. But first I'll be wanting the device you were going to use to corrupt our wormhole stabilizers."

Snipper took the device from his pocket and, making a show of reluctance, gave it to her. He would not be needing it again.

"Cyanne, before we go," said Despina, venturing to speak at last, "what did Woad mean when he said he was going to replace the astronauts on our space station? I ask because two of those astronauts are our friends."

"I'm sorry, Despina, I can't tell you anything more than you already know... No, wait! I *did* hear Lieutenant Lazzuli say something about it. It struck me as a little strange at the time. He said the astronauts had brought 'the instrument of their own destruction' on board. Those were his exact words. Does that help?"

"Yes, I think it does," said Snipper. He smiled at her, though she was still pointing her laser gun at them. "Listen, Cyanne, this is an odd way to part after everything we've been through. But I'd still like to thank you for all you've done - and for giving us the chance to get away. I shan't ever forget."

"Neither shall I," added Despina.

Hearing these kind words, Cyanne looked a little embarrassed but her laser gun remained firmly fixed on the two Earthlings. "I couldn't be a party to murder," she explained. "And I'm sorry I'm to be part of an invasion force. If ever we meet again on Earth, I hope you'll be able to forgive me."

The two Earthlings assured Cyanne they felt only gratitude towards her. Then, without further ado, she escorted them to the lifts. Waiting just out of reach of the CCTV cameras, she gave them their allotted ten minutes to leave the premises and then went off to find Azziur. If he had already reported his suspicions to Woad, there would be no need for her to do so.

Snipper and Despina were not sorry to leave in such a rush, for time was against them. If Woad had not already gathered a search party to look for them, it would not be long before he did so. Once outside, they hurried over to their hover-bike and immediately set off for the lake which they had identified as the location of the test facility. Returning southwards past the valley they had landed in, they spotted the canal feeding the lake and a single lakeside igloo. All was quiet. They hid their hover-bike behind a snowy mound and entered the igloo in silence, their ears pricked for the slightest sound. They had been well briefed for their visit to Mission Control and able to blend into the crowd. But here they were operating blind at a Top Secret facility. Anyone meeting them would be likely to question their presence.

Inside the igloo were glass pods like the ones at Mission Control. This time Snipper did not use the voice samples provided by Peridot. He doubted her defectors had ever heard of the test facility, let alone been given access to it. So instead he used the voices of Woad and Space Marshall Indigo, which he had recorded on his *ubikwe*. It worked. The two Earthlings descended to a cloakroom hung with lab coats and overalls. Snipper noticed there were no boots and the floor was dry. The passageway beyond was empty and, above all, there was no noise. The place seemed deserted.

One by one, they tried all the doors. They went through a series of offices, storerooms and workshops until they found the room they were looking for. It was simply furnished and contained nothing of interest, but the far wall was made entirely of glass. On the other side of the glass were ten Cerulean spacecraft, floating just below the lake's surface and moored to its floor. Each was of a different design but they were all circular, just like Verdissian spacevessels, and one was the spitting image of Rusty. Snipper and Despina stared silently, pondering their next step.

"I can't see any way around it," said Snipper after a few minutes. "We're going to have to board and sabotage all ten vessels one by one.

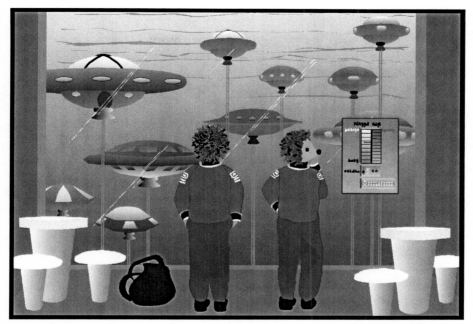

We'll just have to hope the Ceruleans are too busy preparing the invasion fleet to come here. If we want to buy ourselves time, we could try blocking the entrance. But then we'd be trapped inside..."

"There may be another way," said Despina. As a professional hydrologist, she had been thinking the problem through in her own particular way - focussing on the properties of water. "But I'm not sure my Cerulean's good enough for this. I don't want to make any mistakes. Can you translate?" She waved a paw at the control panel set into the glass.

"Of course," said Snipper. He scrutinized the panel. "This twin meter here measures salinity on the left. It's on a descending scale and reading *78 tzels* - but I'm afraid I don't know how to translate that. On the right, you've got a combined figure for surface temperature and wind-chill factor. This time it's on an ascending scale and reading *3 tchils* - that's minus 84° centigrade – I guess it's just as well the heating system on these space suits is so effective. But, look, this is odd: the two needles are level. Do you think that's a coincidence?"

"No, I don't," said Despina. "I think it's meant to be that way. The colder the water, the more salt you need to let in - to stop it from freezing over. When the temperature rises, salt intake is reduced in order to minimize corrosion. The Ceruleans have obviously programmed their machinery to maintain a perfect balance. The question is - is there an over-ride button?"

143

"This one," said Snipper, pointing at a button on the box underneath. "It looks like you press that first and then use the slider to regulate the salt level manually. These rows of buttons here are the intercom and mooring release buttons for each vessel."

"Good - thanks," said Despina. "Now I just need to work out timings. Do you have a piece of paper?"

"A piece of paper?" repeated Snipper, patting his pockets. "You know, I haven't seen a single sheet of the stuff since I left Earth. Maybe they've actually achieved a paperless solar system. No, wait... Here you are." Snipper pulled a crumpled envelope from his trouser pocket. On its front was his home address - 45 Hogarth Avenue, Lairden, Great Bristlin NE1 4TE. Reading it in a far-off galaxy, it seemed strangely incomplete.

Taking the envelope and a pen, Despina now sat down at a table to scribble. She did a few sums, crossed them out and then did a few more, until she had covered the whole envelope.

"That's a pity," she said, half to herself.

"What's a pity?"

"That we can't speed nature up a bit. My idea requires two or three hours to take effect. That may be even slower than boarding each vessel one by one, as you were suggesting. The advantage is we only need a few minutes to set everything in motion. That gives us a much better chance of getting away. And it's not just about saving ourselves - we need to warn everyone back on Earth. We need to warn Pawline and Schnüffel."

"Ideally, yes," agreed Snipper, though he was trying hard not to let his personal feelings intrude. "So what is your idea then?"

"We trap the spacevessels in a layer of ice. All we have to do is release them from their moorings, so they float to the surface, and flush the salt water out of the lake. Then we can go. Nature will take its course. Without any salt in the water, the entire test fleet will be trapped in the ice within an hour. And, as the ice expands around the vessels, they'll start to buckle - they won't have been built to withstand that kind of pressure. Eventually, they'll crack and take on water. Everything inside will be ruined."

"How long will it take to flush the salt water out?"

"Well, the lake's small and shallow. Just looking at it, I'd guess the volume's less than five million cubic metres. So, assuming their systems are at least as good as ours - which of course I do, they're bound to have a filtration rate of at least ten thousand cubic metres per second."

"So that's..."

"Just over eight minutes," said Despina helpfully. "Of course, the plan's not foolproof. If the Ceruleans find out what we've done before the ice has formed, they can simply reverse the process or even move the spacevessels."

"We may be able to delay them," said Snipper. "You could destroy the control panel when you've finished - or will that interfere with the process?"

"Not if I'm careful."

"OK. So, while you're doing that, I'll disable the water taxi - if they can't board the test vessels, they shan't be able to move them either."

"You're very thorough," said Despina, approvingly.

Then, without further ado, she released the spacevessels from their moorings and began the process of flushing the salt water out of the lake. And, when this was finished, she dismantled the control panel so it would be impossible to undo the process. While she was busy doing this, Snipper boarded the water taxi and, firing his laser gun, melted the dashboard.

At last it was time for them to leave. As they exited the lifts, Snipper decided to melt the entry control system, too. Then, while Despina

fetched their transport, he set about destroying the igloo. He was, indeed, very thorough. Nevertheless, when he heard the sound of an approaching hover-bike, he hurried to finish the job. He was surprised Despina had been so quick and he did not turn round immediately. When he did, there was no time to register anything.

Despina saw it all - she was scarcely thirty feet away when it happened. The other hover-bike was going straight for Snipper. She shouted his name but the microphone in her helmet was off. A moment later, the enemy hover-bike had slammed into Snipper, cracking his helmet and knocking him off his feet. As Snipper lay in the snow, struggling to remain conscious, Despina pulled the throttle out and rammed the other hover-bike, throwing the driver from his seat. Then, before the driver could recover, she pulled the semi-conscious Snipper up behind her and was off.

Despina now focussed every fibre of her being on getting away as fast as she could. With the crack in his helmet, Snipper was breathing Cerulean air, getting only half the oxygen he needed. If she did not get him back quickly enough, he would lose consciousness and fall. And, with Woad on their tail, there would be no second chances.

She raced down the valley back towards the coastal plain. Then she made a sharp left turn into the mouth of the neighbouring valley, where Rusty lay waiting for them. They flew over icy rivers, past rock

falls and through snowdrifts. Only as they approached their ravine did Despina look back to check they had not been followed: they were alone. Dipping down into the ravine, she stopped just a foot away from the ring of disturbed snow which marked Rusty's location.

Despina leapt off the hover-bike and slipped her paws under Snipper's arms. He did not respond. "Snipper!" she exclaimed. "Snipper, can you hear me?"

Snipper opened his eyes for a second but then shut them again. Despina knew she would never get him up the ladder in this state. So she opened up Rusty, switched off the invisibility shield and gave Snipper her own helmet. Then, leaving him where he was, she retreated into the spacevessel while she was still able.

Even the short climb back up the ladder left her gasping for air. As she closed the door behind her, leaving him all alone, a terrible fear crept over her. For she had no idea how long he would take to recover. And she knew that time was not on their side. Every now and then, she peered down at him, but there was no sign of movement. And, as she looked out of the window for maybe the tenth time, she spotted a fleet of spacelanders a few miles to the north, shooting up into space from behind the mountain tops. But then at last Snipper stirred. Despina opened the door and called down to him. Staggering to his feet, he pulled himself slowly up the ladder.

"Quickly!" said Despina, helping him in. "We've got to get out of here. Look!"

Snipper closed the door and, collapsing into a chair, took several long deep breaths. "What is it?"

"The Cerulean Space Force," said Despina, hastily switching the invisibility shield back on. "There's a whole fleet of spacelanders taking off. They must have brought everything forward because of us. But at least they won't know what we've done to their ISVs. I suppose they'll only find out when they actually start looking for a wormhole."

"I wouldn't be so sure," said Snipper. "It depends how thorough their pre-flight checks are. Come on, let's get out of here."

The two hedgehogs strapped themselves in and prepared for take-off. Then Snipper pulled a lever, and Rusty sprang up into the sky once more. A few minutes later, he nudged Rusty out of orbit. Then he switched on the autopilot and picked up the manual from under the dashboard.

"What's the matter?" asked Despina.

"Nothing," said Snipper. "I just thought I ought to refresh my memory. After all, I've never done this wormhole business for real before."

Despina nodded. If it had been any other Earthling at the controls, she would have been more worried. But Snipper's ability to master complex alien machinery had already been proven. So, instead of worrying, she sat silently gazing out of the window. To her left, there hovered the fleet of spacelanders which had launched just before them. Beyond that were five vast spaceships, Cerulea's ISVs, which she hoped had now lost their ability for interstellar space travel. Watching them, she expected the spacelanders to make their way back to these mother ships and dock. Yet they did not budge.

"What do you think they're doing?" she asked.

"I'm not sure," said Snipper, looking up, "but I don't much care for their company - even if we are invisible."

"And we may not be as invisible as we think," said Despina. "Even dark matter can be detected by its influence on the visible matter around it."

"All the more reason to put a little distance between us," said Snipper.

So saying, he punched in a set of a random co-ordinates. Then he pulled a lever, propelling Rusty into deep space. As they shot forwards, the Cerulean fleet receded rapidly into the distance. Very

soon the spacelanders had disappeared from view; the much larger ISVs now appeared as a mere pinprick of light in the darkness of space - the light from their solar panels indistinguishable from the light of a distant star.

Snipper switched the autopilot back on and prepared Rusty for intergalactic travel, while Despina prepared lunch. The first step in any intergalactic journey is, of course, the printing and fitting of a fresh wormhole stabilizer. After he had done this, Snipper deployed Rusty's telescope and began to search his monitor for the tell-tale signs of a microscopic wormhole: the wavering light from another solar system or galaxy - or, indeed, just another place - as the wormhole passes in front of it. It was a slow business, requiring intense concentration. So, after lunch, Snipper enlisted Despina's help. Between the two of them, they watched the screen uninterrupted for three hours. But by now both of them were exhausted. Despina suggested they clock off and get a good night's rest.

"I've found one!" exclaimed Snipper suddenly. He locked the telescope's site onto the tiny tear in the fabric of space-time and then fired a barrage of exotic matter straight at it. Looking out the window, Despina could see nothing. But, when she turned to look at the computer screen, she was able to observe a tiny bubble of light grow steadily bigger and bigger. Eventually, it became visible to the naked eye. The two Earthlings watched in fascination as their very own wormhole continued to expand until it was large enough to take a spaceship. Then Snipper engaged the wormhole stabilizer and fired a probe into the now vast wormhole. A second later the probe was back, carrying the data they needed to identify the wormhole's ultimate destination. Sucked back into the spacevessel, the probe popped out into a tray next to the hot drink dispenser. Snipper plugged it into the onboard computer and waited with baited breath, while the computer compared the probe's data with Rusty's own files. After three claw-biting minutes, the results appeared on the screen.

Locality: Asteroid Belt
Solar System: Tiggytwinkle Double Star
Constellation: Hypawshia
Galaxy: Thornton Cluster

The two Earthlings stared at the screen in bitter disappointment. The wormhole would not even take them to their own galaxy, let alone back to Earth. But they had both known the odds of striking lucky first time: looking for their home in this incomprehensibly vast universe was going to be a great deal harder than looking for a needle in a haystack. But needles had been found in haystacks before - the Verdissians and Ceruleans had done it. Snipper and Despina were determined to do it, too. Failure was not an option.

So, after a good night's sleep, they resumed their search. Gradually, they got better at identifying wormholes. Instead of taking three hours to find one, they took just thirty minutes. After two days of searching, they were spotting wormholes at a rate of forty-two an hour. On the seventh day, the results they had been waiting for finally appeared on the screen: Earth. At last they were going home. Snipper propelled Rusty forwards into the gigantic spiral of dust and light.

"No!" protested Despina.

"What is it?"

Snipper was facing the other way but, as he wheeled Rusty round, he saw for himself. A Cerulean spacelander had just followed them into the wormhole.

"I don't believe it!" exclaimed Snipper. "They've tail-gated us." He could not understand how they had spotted the wormhole. After all, the spacelanders were not fitted with wormhole detectors; and the crew could not have seen it with the naked eye from 300 miles away. "Perhaps it's our invisibility shield – perhaps it's malfunctioned."

"But wouldn't they attack if they could see us?" asked Despina.

"No. Thankfully, they need us. If they attacked, they'd risk destroying our wormhole stabilizer. And, without that, the wormhole collapses. ...Mind you," he added, when he had finished checking the monitor for error messages, "the invisibility shield appears to be working fine, so it's got to be something else."

Staring at the spacelander, Snipper began to get the distinct impression of being followed. The spacelander was moving at exactly the same speed as Rusty, maintaining a constant distance. Suddenly it hit him. The Ceruleans had bugged Rusty. Snipper quickly unfolded Rusty's robotic arm.

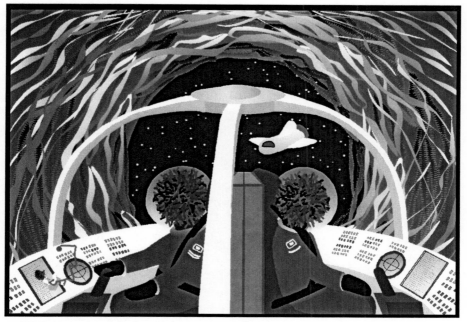

"What are you doing?" asked Despina.

"Ssh!" said Snipper, signalling for to her to be silent. Manoeuvring the camera at the end of the robotic arm, he carefully scanned the vessel's exterior. When he had found the offending item, he brought it inside through the probe hatch and examined it at close quarters. It was roughly the size of a marble, soft and extremely sticky. Snipper peeled back the thick outer layer. Inside - scarcely bigger than a pin head - was a tiny electronic device. He peered at it briefly, then dropped it on the floor and crushed it with his boot, grinding it into smithereens.

"What was that?" asked Despina.

"A tracking device – and probably an eavesdropping device rolled into one. We were being bugged."

"But how did it get there?"

"They must have fired it at us while we had our invisibility shield down. I suppose we're so well insulated in here that's why we never heard it hit. Anyway, let's just thank our lucky stars the glue didn't freeze or we'd never have been able to remove it... Though, now I think of it, they *had* to use a glue which could be deployed in space."

"I'm sorry," said Despina. "It's my fault - I should never have turned off the invisibility shield."

"Don't be sorry," said Snipper. "I really don't think I was in any fit state to climb up an invisible ladder. If it weren't for you, I'd never have made it off Cerulea alive. Anyway, at least the rest of the Cerulean Space Force didn't get through."

"But why didn't they?" asked Despina.

"Well, a wormhole usually stays open for less than a minute, from the point of view of anyone outside it. The Ceruleans must have been pretty quick off the mark even to get one of their spacecraft through. The question is, what will they do once they arrive on the other side? A single spacelander can wreak death and destruction but it's not enough to conquer Earth."

"So they'll try to find us, won't they?" said Despina. "Without Rusty, they'll be stranded in our solar system."

"They will," agreed Snipper, "and that won't do anyone any good."

"Perhaps we can persuade them to go back now, while they still can," suggested Despina.

"I don't know," said Snipper, shaking his head. "If Woad's on board, I doubt he'll listen to reason. Still, I suppose it's worth a try."

Snipper turned on the communications scanner. Within a few seconds, Rusty had located and locked on to a laser beam emanating from the spacelander. Snipper switched the communications channel to open and spoke into the microphone.

"This is Snipper," he announced. "Who am I speaking to?"

"You're speaking to Flight Lieutenant Azziur," came the chilly response. "What do you want?"

"I want to suggest you go home before it's too late," said Snipper, as respectfully as he could: there was nothing to be gained by being rude. "If you follow us through to the other side, there'll be no going back. And, though we wish you no ill, after all that's happened you won't be welcome on Earth."

"We do not seek a welcome from you," said Azziur. "We seek only your spacevessel. When we come out the other side of the wormhole, you're to dock at your space station. We shall then come and collect your vessel."

"Out of the question," said Snipper. "You must know by now that we're not the fools you thought we were. Why would we destroy your wormhole capability, only to give it back to you?"

"To save your friends," said another voice. It was Commander Woad. Little shivers ran down Snipper's spines. "Unless you give us your spacevessel, all the astronauts on board your space station will be exterminated. Perhaps you don't believe me - "

"On the contrary," said Snipper, for he remembered Woad's speech back on Cerulea all too well. "But I happen to know you were already planning to kill the astronauts. Why should I believe you won't kill us all anyway?"

"The choice is yours," said Woad. "And you can have a good long think about it while you travel through the wormhole. Just remember this. If you make the wrong decision, you'll have Earthling blood on your paws. *You* will be responsible for Pawline's and Schnüffel's deaths."

Part 3

Chapter Thirteen

Pawline woke at 6 a.m. to the sound of *Mr Spacehog* playing over the loudspeaker. She smiled. It was her fourth morning on board the space station, and today she would carry out her very first spacewalk. It was the moment she had been waiting for all her life. But then she remembered the Verdissian threat and her friends, lost in space. With the thought that she would probably never see them again, her mood quickly changed. It had been like that every morning - happiness followed by heartache. But still she had maintained her focus. She had trained for this mission for nearly three years. And a great many other hedgehogs had worked long and hard to put her into space: she was not going to let them down now. As for the lurking threat of an alien attack, it only went to prove just how important her work in space was. For now, more than ever, Earthlings needed to understand the universe around them.

Pawline wished her fellow astronaut Hejji as cheery a good morning as she could muster. The two of them had camped out in the depressurized airlock overnight, in order to prepare their bodies for the near vacuum of space. But now it was time for their morning wash and breakfast. So the two hedgehogs unzipped their sleeping bags and, with oxygen masks on, repressurized the airlock. When it was equal with the rest of the space station, they unsealed the inner hatch and drifted over to the bathroom. At 6:40 precisely - for they operated to a strict timetable - they joined Schnüffel and the other astronauts in the kitchen. Fuzz, Spurrov and Ilexei were all in high spirits. Somehow they had learned to ignore the Verdissian threat – it seemed nothing could dampen their natural enthusiasm for long.

After a simple rehydrated breakfast, the two spacewalkers returned to the airlock with Schnüffel and Fuzz, who helped them into their space suits. This took some time, as the suits were complex and bulky. Back on Earth, they would barely have been able to stand up under the weight, but here they were weightless; and, on a spacewalk, they were essential to an astronaut's survival, carrying everything from oxygen and a jetpack to protection against micrometeoroids.

Once fully suited, Pawline and Hejji were left to wait on their own in the airlock, while the pressure was reduced again. This was done to prevent them being sucked out when the hatch was finally opened. They also tethered themselves to each other; and Pawline, who was to be last out, attached herself to a rail inside the airlock. Now they were ready to go. Hejji opened the small round hatch and exited carefully, feet first. When he had locked onto the outside rail, Pawline followed.

For a minute or so, she was so focussed on her exit that all she saw was the hatch and the exterior of the space station. But, once clear, she

155

finally noticed the view. And, though she had already spent many happy minutes gazing out of the space station cupola, the view from outside was of an entirely different order. The colours of her planet and the immensity of the universe struck her as they had never done before.

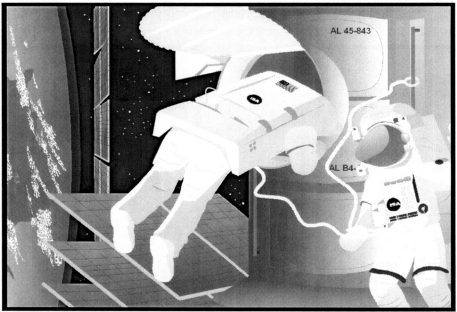

But there was work to be done. Hejji went off to remove a sun shield from an extremophile experiment, while Pawline made her way over to the alpha magnetic spectrometer - the giant magnet Snipper had once asked her about. Her task was to check and record its condition after its first six months in space. It was an astronomically expensive piece of equipment, so she was anxious to see it had come to no harm. She photographed it thoroughly from all angles. And, when she was halfway through, she was about to report her progress to Mission Control in Hogston, back in the United Stakes; but, before she could do so, Schnüffel's voice came through her headset.

"Hogston, we have a problem," he said. Speaking quietly and clearly, he sounded calm; but astronauts are trained to be that way. "It looks like a computer malfunction. All life support systems are down - oxygen generators, carbon dioxide scrubbers, cooling system - everything. Over."

"OK, Schnüffel, thanks for that," said Hogston, sounding equally calm. "Yeah, we're getting the same reading down here. Have you tried switching it off and on again...? Right, yeah, I thought you might have. Well, we'll take a look and get back to you. Hejji and Pawline, how are you two doing? "

"The spectrometer's looking good," said Pawline. "I should be done photographing it in another ten minutes."

"OK, Pawline. When you've finished, proceed to the damaged solar panel as planned. There's nothing to be gained from cancelling your spacewalk now. On the contrary, while we're sorting this problem out, it's best if we keep the number of hedgehogs on board to a minimum. How about you, Hejji? How's it going?"

"It's going great, thanks. The sun shield's off; now I'm fixing the cabling."

"Good, it sounds like you're both doing just fine. Speak to you all later. Over and out."

Pawline carried on with her photography. Like the others, she remained calm. There would be plenty of time to fix the malfunction before the oxygen ran out or carbon dioxide levels rose too high. Furthermore, there was a whole team of hedgehogs working on the problem back on Earth - and they were among the best minds in the world. Knowing all this, she was able to work undisturbed. And, when Hogston spoke again, she rather expected the news to be good.

"Earth calling Schnüffel - Hogston here. Look, we're still working on your computer malfunction, but I'm afraid there's a new problem -

157

an ammonia leak. You'll need to seal off the forward segment and put on your oxygen masks."

"Understood," said Schnüffel. "Fuzz, can you deal with that, please? So, Hogston, can you tell where the leak's coming from?"

"Well, that's just it. Our readings suggest all ten heat exchangers may be leaking."

"All ten?" repeated Schnüffel, sounding puzzled. "Are you sure? Is that actually possible?"

"If it's happened, it's possible," said Hogston. Then a note of unease crept into his voice. "Look, I don't know how to break this to you, but we're either real unlucky today... or this was no accident."

For a moment there was radio silence. The astronauts' training was so thorough; it prepared them for every conceivable emergency - for everything except a deliberate act of sabotage. Shivers ran down Pawline's spines at the mere thought of it.

"Could you repeat that, please?" asked Schnüffel, "We're not sure we heard you correctly."

"No, you heard me right the first time," said Hogston. "This looks like a case of sabotage. I'll be frank, it could have been done from down here or it could even have been one of you. But just let's keep cool, let's solve the problem and let's not make it any worse by guessin'."

"Of course," said Schnüffel, though he did not much like the suggestion that one of his fellow astronauts might be responsible. He was about to say so, when another voice came over the radio.

"Pawline, are you there? Can you hear me? Pawline?"

Schnüffel did not recognize the voice. Even Pawline hesitated, scarcely able to believe her ears. Indeed, it was a voice neither of them had really expected they would ever hear again.

"Pawline, it's Snipper here - can you hear me? Can *anyone* hear me?"

"Snipper!" said Pawline at last, breathless with emotion. "Is that... is that really you?"

"Where are you?" asked Schnüffel. "What planet are you on? Or are you still on the spaceship?"

"I'm on the spaceship," said Snipper, not bothering to explain that he had been on more than one. "I should be with you in under fifteen minutes."

"What about Despina?" asked Pawline.

"She's here with me - she's fine. Now I need you both to listen. Do you remember, Pawline, that text about Count de Poynte which was sent from my phone? Well, it wasn't me who sent it but de Poynte, himself. Or I should say Commander Woad, because that's his real name. I scarcely remember the details of what he said - but then I suppose it was about six months ago - "

"Six months?" repeated Pawline. "You mean three weeks ago."

"Well, yes and no," said Snipper, rather confusingly; but right now he did not have time to explain the complexities of wormhole travel. "The important thing to understand," he continued, "is the text was full of lies. Woad and his Ceruleans are the threat, not the Verdissians."

"Snipper, be careful!" said Pawline. "Didn't you say you were still on Woad's spaceship? Won't he be listening in on this?"

"No, I'm not on *his* spaceship – not any more. Though he may be listening in. If he is, it can't be helped. I'm afraid he's not far behind us. We're just a little bit faster than he is. Which brings me to the point - he wants us to give him Rusty, our spacevessel."

"Snipper, this is Hogston speaking. Sorry to interrupt, but we have been fully briefed - Schnüffel and Pawline have told us everything they know. Now did you say.... *your* spacevessel?"

"Well, sort of ours - it's a long story. The key point is Woad's threatening to kill everyone on board the space station unless we give him Rusty - and we can't. Giving Rusty to the Ceruleans would give them back the wormhole capability they've just lost. And, as soon as they're able to resume interstellar space travel, they'll launch a full-scale invasion of Earth. So, you see, us holding onto Rusty's the only thing standing in their way. I hate to say this, but you need to evacuate the space station - now."

"Hold on a moment," said Hogston. "Did Woad say *how* he was going to carry out his threat? The space station's already experiencing some serious problems - ammonia leaks, life support systems down; and everything points to sabotage. But we can sort this out. We've sealed off the danger zone and the astronauts all have oxygen masks, so they're not in any imminent danger. If Woad *is* responsible and that's all he's got up his sleeve, we'll be OK."

"No, he'll have more - you can be sure of that," said Snipper. "And he's on his way here right now. Look, I may be able to help with these problems you mention. But, in the meantime, you *must* get ready to evacuate."

"All right then," said Hogston. "Schnüffel, you know what to do."

"Understood," said Schnüffel. "Pawline and Hejji, you'd better finish up and return to the airlock at once. I'll wait for you there. Fuzz, Ilexei, Spurrov, prepare to evacuate... Now, Snipper, what can you tell us about our ammonia leaks and the computer malfunctions?"

"Just this: one of the Ceruleans said you'd brought the instrument of your own destruction on board. Those were his exact words. So something must have been brought up in the shuttle which they've used to attack the space station's systems. And I reckon I can narrow it down still further, because I happen to know they've been inside the Astellaritz space factory."

"Did you say Astellaritz?" said Pawline, who was still listening as she made her way back towards the airlock. "Woad must have been talking about our on-board robot."

"No, it can't be that," said Schnüffel. "Robohog isn't connected to our computers. And he wouldn't plug himself in - he isn't programmed to do that."

"Actually, I think Pawline may be right," said Snipper. "Robohog may not have been designed that way, but these Ceruleans could easily have modified his programming. Technologically speaking, I'm afraid they're simply light years ahead of us."

"All right, point taken," said Schnüffel. "I'll go and check on him. It won't take long."

For a short while there was radio silence, as they all went about their business. Off air, Despina asked Snipper how long he thought it would take before Woad was in firing range of the space station.

"I don't know," said Snipper. "He may even be in range right now, but he can't afford to open fire. After all, we won't give him Rusty if he's just murdered our friends and left us nowhere to transfer to."

161

"But you've already refused him Rusty. Perhaps you should have played along."

"I thought of it," said Snipper. "But he wouldn't have believed me. No one would give in that quickly."

"Hogston? Snipper? It's Schnüffel here. I've found Robohog - and Pawline was right. He's shut himself in the aft airlock and he's depressurizing. He seems to be preparing to go outside."

"Or maybe he's planning to open both hatches," suggested Snipper. "The inner and outer at the same time. Is that possible?"

"No, thank goodness," said Schnüffel. "There are safety measures in place to prevent that."

"But what if he overrides those measures?"

"It's a physical impossibility," insisted Schnüffel.

"That's what they said about wormhole travel," said Despina.

"Well then," said Schnüffel grimly, "if we're still on board when he does it, we'll be sucked out into space. And, without space suits, we'll die. Frankly, even with them, it would only be a matter of time if we couldn't come back."

"Correct," said a new and unwelcome voice. "This is Commander Woad of the Cerulean Space Force speaking. Robohog has indeed been upgraded and is now under my control. You've already seen a demonstration of his capabilities. For you were right to think it was Robohog that turned off your life support systems and caused the ammonia leaks. And now, if Snipper continues to refuse my demands, Robohog *will* open both hatches. Everyone on board will die."

"Snipper's told us about you," said Schnüffel. "If he gives you his spacevessel, that won't be the end of it. We know about the Ceruleans' plan to invade Earth."

"Snipper's being unreasonable," responded Woad. "Without a wormhole-enabled spacecraft, my crew and I will be stranded in your solar system. Is that what you want?"

"No," said Snipper truthfully. "But you've got to give us time to reach the space station. We have to have somewhere to go."

"Naturally," said Woad. "But you must drop your invisibility shield so we can see where you are. We shall then decide for ourselves exactly how much time you need."

"Very well," said Snipper. He looked at Despina, asking for her approval. She nodded, and he pressed the button.

Though Pawline was still outside the space station, she never noticed the sudden appearance of Snipper's flying saucer above them.

She had just one thing on her mind - to stop Robohog. None of the astronauts inside the station could reach him now. And, of the two spacewalkers, she was the nearest. So she ignored the instruction to return to the forward airlock and instead continued to the rear of the space station. Activating her emergency jetpack, she propelled herself along the main body of the station to the aft airlock. The outer hatch was open. Peering inside, she saw Robohog with his back turned to her. He was staring in through the tiny window of the inner hatch. Schnüffel was on the other side.

Pawline did not fancy a tussle with Robohog in the confined space of the airlock. Enormously strong, with highly flexible arm-like legs and no space suit to slow him down, he would be far more agile than her. He could easily damage her life support systems. It would be far better if she could lure him away from the space station. So, staying outside, she pushed the outer hatch to and waited, hoping he would notice and come after her.

It did not take long for the hatch to swing open again and Robohog's head to appear, searching for the culprit. When he spotted her, he pulled himself through the outer hatch and clamped his feet onto the nearest rail. She immediately propelled herself in his direction, only to be flung away like a hoglet's unwanted toy. With nothing to grab hold of, she flew off into the dark void, only stopping when she came to the end of her tether. Then, as quickly as she could, she began to reel herself in. But, before she had finished, Robohog unhooked her from the space station. The emergency jetpack was now her only lifeline. Firing on this, she made one final dive for Robohog and tore open the flap in his side. As she pulled his switch, he seized her arm. A second later, he had stopped dead in his tracks, but Pawline was trapped - caught in his vice-like grip.

"Pawline? Hejji?" It was Schnüffel speaking. "What's happening out there? I just saw..." He stopped himself mid-sentence. He had just seen Robohog depart but was reluctant to share this information with Woad, who would certainly be listening.

"I've turned off Robohog," said Pawline. "I tricked him into following me out of the airlock. I guess the Ceruleans didn't make him so very smart after all - if he'd understood the hatch couldn't be locked from the outside, he would have ignored me. The only problem is he grabbed my arm and now I'm stuck."

"Are you OK?" asked Hogston.

"Yeah, I'm OK," she responded, sounding surprisingly relaxed. But a moment later she spoke again - still sounding calm but now with a note of urgency in her voice: "No, scrub that - I spoke too soon. He's torn my sleeve. Hold on a moment while I have a look… Yeah, my air supply's dropping - and fast. I reckon I've got... Well, at this rate I've got just under thirteen minutes' supply left."

"Hang on in there, Pawline," said Hogston. "Hejji, how quickly can you get to her with your toolbox?"

"I'll be there in five."

"Right," said Hogston. "So, add to that another fifteen to dismantle Robohog's arm..." His voice tailed off halfway through his sentence.

"All right, Hogston, I can do the math," said Pawline, calmly enough. "Hejji, any chance you can speed it up?"

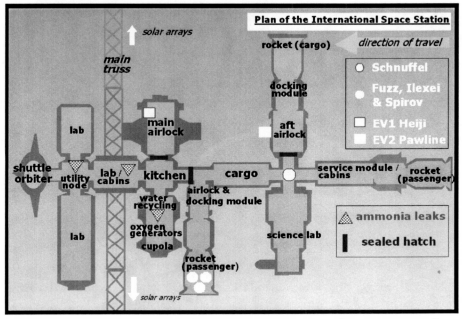

"Don't worry, Pawline," said Snipper. "*We're* coming to get you."

Twisting her head round, Pawline finally noticed the small red flying saucer hurrying towards the space station. As it grew closer, she even recognized her friends inside it.

"This changes nothing!" shouted Woad, unable to hide his anger. "If Snipper doesn't give me his spacevessel, I'll just shoot your space station out of the sky! Snipper, you've got five minutes to dock and join your friends."

"All right, you win!" said Snipper. "You can have our spacevessel. But we're rescuing Pawline first – that's not negotiable. And you know five minutes isn't enough."

Despina looked at her watch. Pawline had eleven minutes left before the air ran out.

"Very well," said Woad. "Rescue your friend. But I'm watching you."

165

Snipper slowed down to a snail's pace as he approached Pawline. Then he unfolded Rusty's robotic arm and used it to grab hold of Robohog's arm. Carefully - as slowly as he dared with just eight minutes to play with - he wrenched it from its socket. Pawline was free, though now with just four minutes' air left and Robohog's arm still attached to her own. Squeezing into the airlock as fast as she could, she sealed it behind her.

"Now," said Woad, "no more delays. You dock and transfer immediately, Snipper, or else..."

"How do we know you won't destroy the space station once Snipper and Despina are on board?" asked Schnüffel.

"You don't," said Woad with a sneer. "But, if Snipper doesn't keep his word, you can be sure I will."

"I *will* keep my word," said Snipper, though as he spoke he racked his brains for a way out. He wondered if he could somehow place Rusty between Woad and the space station. Yet he knew he could not shield the whole of its vast structure. Reluctantly, he steered Rusty towards the forward docking module.

"Snipper, stay where you are!" said a female voice he had not heard before. "Woad's not to be trusted."

"Who's that?" asked Snipper. Instinctively, he turned his head - just in time to see a large Verdissian spacecraft appear as though from nowhere.

"This is Captain Minty of the Verdissian Space Force speaking. We'll not tolerate these threats to the Earthlings, Commander Woad. You must leave them in peace. Our offer of a home on Verdis still stands - though you've done nothing to deserve it. In the meantime, we shall escort you back through the wormhole ourselves and ensure your safe return to Cerulea."

"What?" exploded Woad. "You dare interfere in the operations of the Cerulean Space Force? I'll not be dictated to by a Verdissian. Neither will I be refused by a mere Earthling. Snipper, you have a clear choice - surrender now or watch your friends die!"

"But, Commander Woad, that spacevessel you're after doesn't belong to Snipper. It belongs to Dr Peridot of the Verdissian Space Force. Taking it would be an act of piracy against Verdissian property."

"Nonsense!" said Woad. "It ceased to be a Verdissian spacevessel as soon as your Dr Peridot gave it to an Earthling. Snipper, you have two minutes. If you haven't surrendered by then, Flight Lieutenant Azziur will open fire on the space station."

"No, Commander Woad, I will not," said Azziur. "You've gone too far this time. You must be out of your mind to provoke the Verdissians like this. I'm relieving you of your command."

"What? Is this mutiny? Sapphire, arrest the traitor and kill the Earthlings! Exterminate them! Do you hear me, Sapphire? Do as I say!"

"It's no good, sir," said Azziur. "Sapphire will take her orders from me now. Our mission has failed. Killing the Earthlings now would be illogical. It would serve no purpose other than to satisfy your thirst for revenge. And do you really think you can destroy them in full view of the Verdissians and get away with it? How can we even justify such an action to ourselves? Snipper has shown us what Earthlings are truly made of, but you shame us all with your barbarity. Sapphire, take him away!"

"No!" shouted Woad. "Take your paws off me at once!" He continued to protest but gradually his voice tailed away until he was heard no more.

"Snipper?" It was Azziur speaking again. "Can you hear me?"

"I hear you," said Snipper cautiously. He wondered whether he should believe what he heard or whether this was another Cerulean trick.

"It's over," said Azziur, and he sounded as though he really meant it. "He... *We* shall not be troubling you again. Captain Minty, if you'd be so kind, we'd like to go home."

Epilogue

Snipper and Despina wanted to go home, too. But they waited around long enough to see the Ceruleans and Verdissians enter the wormhole which would take them back to their own solar system. Only when they saw the wormhole close behind them could they finally relax. As the Ceruleans departed, Azziur repeated his promise that they would not attempt to return; and Captain Minty promised to make sure they did not. The Earthlings in their turn expressed their profound gratitude to the Verdissians. Snipper even softened a little towards Azziur, whose new-found humility came as something of a surprise; but he could not forget his complicity in the plot to murder Despina. Cyanne was the only Cerulean to come out of this business truly well. She had risked as much as anyone, though personally she had stood to gain nothing by helping hedgehogs from another planet. Snipper wanted to know she had come to no harm for her trouble; he asked Azziur whether the crew he had travelled out with were all well; Azziur was a little surprised he should care but assured him they were. And, if only Snipper could have seen it, he would have been delighted to know that Cyanne would not only live a long and prosperous life, but her strength of character would lead her on to great things in years to come.

When the wormhole finally closed, one Verdissian remained behind - or two, to be more exact. For Captain Minty had sent Peridot back down to Earth to find their long-lost colleague and friend, Lieutenant Kloraphyll. After a thorough check of the hospitals in and around Milchnicht, Peridot finally located her. Against the odds, Kloraphyll had survived what should have been a lethal dose of poison - most probably thanks to the effects of Earth's very different climate. More than that, in the three weeks since the Verdissian evacuation, she had made a full recovery. Peridot's own expert medical examination revealed only the faintest traces of poison. Indeed, it was only the return of Kloraphyll's natural colouring that had kept her in hospital so long. The Earthling doctors had never seen anything like it. They watched with growing alarm as, every day, she turned a little greener; and they examined her over and over again. Thankfully, they failed to find the cause, since the patient so steadfastly refused to undergo a blood test. But, being unable to return to her flat, she was also unable to remedy the situation - for this was where her supplies of *brunnetinctus* were all stored. Naturally, her attempts to contact the rest of her landing party failed. The communication lines had gone dead, for they had vanished off the face of the Earth. Then, just as she was becoming quite desperate, Peridot turned up. Within an hour, three bottles of *brunnetinctus* had been smuggled into the hospital; and, within two days, Kloraphyll was back to 'normal'. Finally, she was allowed to go home.

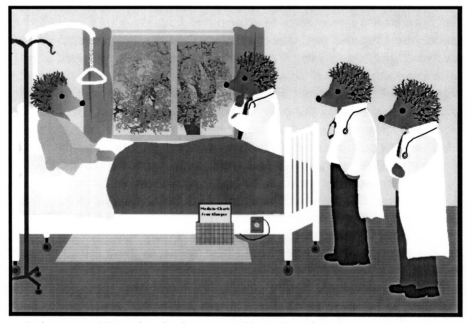

Snipper and Despina had meanwhile delayed their own return home for one more day, so they could join their friends on board the international space station for a little celebration. For, by now, all systems had been restored, and Pawline and Hejji were safely back inside. Deploying Rusty's adjustable docking gear, Snipper docked onto the space station right next to the space shuttle orbiter which had brought Pawline and Schnüffel up from Earth. And, as Snipper opened the hatch on his side, Pawline opened the hatch on hers. Face-to-face again at last, the two friends greeted each other with the warmest of hugs. A moment later, Despina and Schnüffel had joined in this joyful reunion. Finally, Hejji, Fuzz, Ilexei and Spurrov were introduced to the visitors, and there were hugs, paw shakes and expressions of delight all round. Before long, the astronauts were wandering over to have their first ever look inside an alien spacecraft. Then Snipper and Despina were given a full tour of the space station. They were shown everything from the tiny cupboard-like sleeping cabins to the science labs, with their sophisticated equipment and numerous experiments. And, for all the astonishing and wonderful things they had seen over the last few months, they were genuinely impressed - because after all they, too, were Earthlings; in their eyes, nothing could diminish the achievements of their fellows. The tour concluded with a simple rehydrated supper, washed down with a celebratory fruit punch. Then songs were sung, Pawline produced a ukulele, and Despina was persuaded to accompany them all on the resident keyboard.

Eventually, however, it really was time to go home, for Snipper and Despina were expecting visitors. So, after a good night's sleep, Snipper undocked Rusty for the last time and flew them directly to his flat; travelling in this speedy Verdissian spacevessel, it was a journey of just twenty minutes. On reaching his back garden, he hovered for a minute or so, carefully adjusting his position. And, looking down, he was surprised to see how much autumn colour there still was. But, while the travellers had experienced an absence of six months, the calendar had moved forward less than one. And, though it was a little disconcerting for them, they were thankful. It would save them from too many awkward questions.

Snipper landed the tiny spacevessel on his patio. With the invisibility shield up, none of his neighbours noticed the arrival. Yet

landing an alien spacecraft in such familiar surroundings was perhaps the strangest experience of the last six months. It was also the happiest.

Then, for one day, life returned to normal. Of course, its very normality felt strange, after everything Snipper and Despina had been through and with a new life together to look forward to. Yet they took a great deal of pleasure in everyday chores - as they put on the washing, restocked the fridge and dusted the place thoroughly. And, by the time the doorbell rang, the flat was spotless and welcoming; there were flowers in every room, candles on the mantelpiece and a fire burning in the grate. Peridot and Kloraphyll - for they were the visitors - were delighted. Though they had spent several months on Earth, they had never before been invited into an Earthling's home. Snipper and Despina did their very best to make their short stay a memorable one. They showed them the sites, took them for a walk in the country and treated them to a traditional Sunday lunch at Snipper's favourite country pub. They even went to a concert - though the subject of Despina's interrupted performance at the Palace Museum was tactfully avoided.

When the time came for the visitors to go, there was sadness on both sides, for they knew they would not meet again. Though the Verdissians had retained their wormhole technology, they were too concerned about the risks involved to plan any further visits to Earth. So they said their goodbyes. Then the two Verdissians vanished as they stepped inside the invisibility shield surrounding Rusty. Though there was little to see, Snipper and Despina remained on the balcony to wave goodbye. They watched as a flurry of leaves flew up from the garden and knew what it meant: Peridot, Kloraphyll and Rusty were gone.

Following the Verdissians' departure, Snipper and Despina were summoned to a series of secret meetings, where they were thoroughly questioned about their experiences. A detailed account of everything that had happened was gradually built up, recorded, stamped *Top Secret* and then filed under layer upon layer of security. Finally, the two of them were sworn to secrecy - just as everyone else involved in the affair had been, from astronauts to politicians. For no one else was ever to be allowed to know the truth - that Earth had once been visited by hedgehogs from outer space.

Postscript:
the facts behind *Hedgehogs from Outer Space*

The universe inhabited by Snipper and his companions has more in common with our own than you might think. So you may be interested to read the following facts about human space exploration, science and technology and about hibernation as currently practised by hedgehogs, dormice and bats.

The International Space Station, the Space Shuttle and Astronauts

The **International Space Station** (ISS) is the largest spacecraft ever built. Measuring 356 feet wide by 240 feet long (109 metres by 73 metres), it houses four laboratories and, at any one time, around 150 science experiments and usually six astronauts. It is truly international - the work of five space agencies[1] and sixteen countries - and an extraordinary example of what can be achieved through co-operation.

The ISS has to travel at a speed of five miles per second (8km) to stay in orbit around Earth (rather than crashing down onto it or disappearing off into outer space)[2]. This means it circles the world sixteen times a day. When it passes overhead on a clear night, it is visible to the naked eye even though it is 250 miles up (400km); what you see is sunlight reflected off its enormous solar panels. Have a look at NASA's[3] website to find out when it will be passing over your neighbourhood.

Various different spacecraft have been used to ferry astronauts, cargo and components up to the ISS. The USA's contribution was the famous **Space Shuttle**, a partially reusable spacecraft which carried between two and eleven people. In 2011, the Space Shuttle fleet was retired after thirty years of service. Currently, all travel to the ISS is on board the Russian Soyuz, which carries three people (there are usually two Soyuz docked onto the ISS). Cargo vessels carrying supplies of fuel, food, water, experiments and spare parts are supplied by Europe, Japan, Russia and the USA.

---

[1] The five agencies are NASA (USA), Roscosmos (Russia), JAXA (Japan), CSA (Canada) and ESA (Europe).
[2] The speed required to stay in orbit is called "orbital velocity". This is achieved when linear speed exactly equals the downward force of gravity.
[3] NASA is the National Aeronautics and Space Administration. It is the USA's space agency.

173

Constructed between 1998 and 2011, the ISS has been continuously occupied since 2000. The **astronauts** on board do a full working week (thirty-five hours), running experiments and looking after the ISS. They also get to enjoy fantastic views of the Earth, see a sunrise every forty-five minutes and experience the sensation of weightlessness. (This sensation results from the fact that the astronauts, the ISS itself and everything inside it are all free-falling at the same speed.[4])

Becoming an astronaut takes many years of hard work with no guarantee of success. Just to apply, you must have studied engineering, medicine or a science. Astronauts need to be healthy. They need to speak Russian and English. They also need to be good at getting on with other people: they often spend up to six months together in the confined space of the ISS; and, in March 2015, two astronauts began the first ever year-long stay there.

All astronauts either come from a country with a space programme or are privately funded. Since 2002, the European Space Agency (ESA)[5] has had a single European Astronaut Corps, which has its home base at the European Astronaut Centre in Germany[6]. On 15th December 2015, Timothy Peake becomes the first Briton to fly in space as a member of the ESA.[7]

Munich, Space Technology and Robots

Milchnicht, where *Hedgehogs from Outer Space* opens, bears a strong resemblance to **Munich**, the capital of Bavaria in Germany. A city of medieval origin, Munich has many attractive buildings. Its Residenz (similar to the Palace Museum in Snipper's story) was formerly the palace of Bavarian kings and is now a museum; concerts

---

[4] Although gravity weakens as you get further away from the Earth, on the ISS it still retains 90% of the force you experience on the ground, so this is *not* the reason for the feeling of weightlessness. Free-falling is falling without the sensation of any counteracting force. Sky-divers free-fall before they open their parachutes. At funfairs people briefly free-fall when they go over the crest of a roller-coaster.

[5] The ESA's members are Austria, Belgium, the Czech Republic, Denmark, Estonia, Finland, France, Germany, Greece, Hungary, Ireland, Italy, Luxembourg, the Netherlands, Norway, Poland, Portugal, Romania, Spain, Sweden, Switzerland and the United Kingdom.

[6] All astronauts bound for the ISS spend time at the European Astronaut Centre in order to learn about the European-built parts of the ISS. This includes non-European astronauts.

[7] The UK's first astronaut was Helen Sharman in 1991, who was privately funded and flew on a Russian Soyuz. The four who followed her had American as well as British passports: they flew with NASA as US nationals. To learn more about the UK's current space-related work, visit www.gov.uk/government/organisations/uk-space-agency.

are sometimes held in its chapel. Munich is also famous for its annual folk festival, the Oktoberfest, which runs from late September to early October; many people dress up in traditional German folk costume for this. South of the city lie the beautiful Bavarian lakes; among these is Chiemsee, whose second largest island, Fraueninsel, is similar to Igelininsel in Snipper's story.

Just outside the city is a **German Aerospace** (DLR) research centre, which works with space missions and develops advanced robotics. Robots developed at this site will soon be sent into space to take on dangerous tasks currently performed by astronauts; there is even a project to build a robot which can travel thousands of miles on its own and repair remote satellites. However, the robot currently working alongside the astronauts on board the ISS was built by the US space agency, NASA. Known as **"Robonaut"** (and strikingly similar to Robohog), it was designed as a humanoid so it could carry out simple, repetitive or particularly dangerous tasks currently undertaken by astronauts.

Also at the DLR site is the Columbus Control Centre, known by its call-sign Col-CC, which is connected up with the ISS mission control centres in Houston (USA) and Moscow (Russia); Col-CC is responsible for operations inside "Columbus", the ISS's European laboratory, and for all the European experiments and equipment on board the ISS.

The Universe

Are we alone in the universe? No one knows. Of the eight planets orbiting the star we call the Sun, only Earth is capable of supporting life. But you only have to look up into the night sky to see thousands more stars besides our own[8]; and, with the aid of telescopes, astronomers have mapped millions. Any planets orbiting these stars are inevitably a great deal harder to see, as planets do not emit light. Until recently, it was not actually known for certain that there *were* any planets beyond our own solar system. But, since the first confirmed discovery in 1992, almost two thousand planets have been spotted. The number continues to grow.

---

[8] This should be in as dark a spot as you can manage - well away from street lighting. In a city you may only be able to see about 30 stars on a clear night.

Do any of these planets support life? On Earth liquid water is essential to life, so scientists are searching for planets where this might exist - rocky planets neither too close to nor too far from their star. Other conditions necessary for life on Earth include: its molten core, as the source of all geothermal activity; the magnetic field which shields us from the solar wind; and its atmosphere, which provides further protection and helps keep us warm. Scientists are also searching for planets showing gases such as oxygen and methane, as these are released into the atmosphere by living creatures.

Interstellar Travel

If scientists do identify planets which could support life, those planets will unfortunately be too far away for us Earthlings to visit and check. The nearest star to our own, Proxima Centauri, is 4.2 light years away. A light year is the distance light travels in one year, which is 5,878,499,810,000 miles (9,460,528,400,000km). The fastest outward-bound spacecraft in human history, Voyager 1, is moving at 38,610 mph (62,140 kmph). At this rate, it would take Voyager 1 80,000 years to reach Proxima Centauri.

Various ideas have been suggested for getting around this problem. One is the use of shortcuts called "**wormholes**" (you may remember that Cyanne described these as "tiny, microscopic holes in the fabric of space-time"). However, although the existence of wormholes is indicated by mathematics[9], no human scientist has ever observed one or proven their existence. If they *do* exist, using them as a means of travel is likely to be either impossible or very, very difficult; and, if travel through them *is* possible, it will be highly dangerous - carrying the risk of sudden collapse and high radiation.

On the other hand, trying to work out what will (or will not) be possible in the future is almost impossible itself. Imagine you were around in 1903, when the world's first powered aircraft flew ten feet off the ground for twelve seconds and that seemed a remarkable achievement. Would you have believed it possible to send a spacecraft to the edge of our solar system and beyond? Probably not. Yet this was achieved on 25th August 2012, when Voyager 1 crossed from our solar system into interstellar space - the "space between the stars".[10]

---

[9] Wormholes were predicted by Einstein's theory of general relativity.
[10] Interstellar space is the place where the sun's flow of material and magnetic field stop affecting its surroundings. Voyager 1 was launched in 1977 and, as of 2015, has travelled

Hibernation

Another significant problem connected with any kind of long-distance spaceflight is the effect upon astronauts' minds and bodies, plus the enormous supplies needed to support life. Even a mission to neighbouring Mars will be problematic, as it still involves a twelve-month round trip plus stopover time. Yet NASA is planning just such a mission for the 2030s. It is therefore exploring various possible solutions, one of which is hibernation. Of course, hibernation would have to be artificially induced as, unlike hedgehogs, we are not able to do it naturally. NASA is looking for ways to achieve this. In the meantime, hedgehogs, dormice and bats are the only indigenous British species to hibernate.

So what exactly is hibernation? Though often thought of as a kind of deep sleep, it is actually much more complex than that. The purpose of sleep is rest and recuperation, which are essential to survival. The purpose of hibernation is the conservation of energy, and the need for it depends upon exterior conditions. In winter, when food sources are scarce, a hedgehog risks expending more energy looking for food than he (or she) gains from eating. So he allows his temperature to fall from 35°C to between 1 and 10°C (from 95°F to between 34 and 50°F). This means that other functions also have to slow down, including breathing and heart rate. But it conserves energy and there may be further advantages. Scientific studies have shown that small hibernating mammals generally have longer life spans, and this is thought to be due in part to slower ageing.[11]

Although hibernation saves about 90% of a hedgehog's energy, he will still lose around 20-25% of his body weight during this time. So he must prepare by fattening up. Weight is built up gradually over the spring and summer, but it is particularly important to get enough to eat in the weeks running up to hibernation (the Ceruleans' week-long "Hibernival" would not be enough for *our* hedgehogs). This added

---

12,000,000,000 miles (20,000,000,000 km) from Earth. It will stop transmitting in the 2020s, when it runs out of fuel, but will go on travelling at the same speed forever.

[11] See *Hibernation is associated with increased survival and the evolution of slow life histories among mammals* by Christopher Turbill, Claudia Bieber and Thomas Ruf, published online by rspb.royalsocietypublishing.org: this found that life spans were 50% greater for a 50g (1.8oz) species. However, it should be borne in mind that hedgehogs typically weigh 600-900g.

weight then not only supports the remaining bodily activity but also allows him to generate heat when the time comes to wake up.

Also by Elizabeth Morley

Let Sleeping Hedgehogs Spy

Let Sleeping Hedgehogs Spy is Snipper's first adventure. As the story opens, he is looking forward to a skiing holiday away from it all with his friends; but a sinister plot is afoot and their holiday is disrupted when he finds himself pitted against a criminal mastermind known only as "Mr E".

Snipper is soon on Mr E's tail. But along the way he must protect his friends, hide his own identity and decide once and for all whether the hedgehog in blue is friend or foe. Perhaps she is nothing to do with Mr E. Perhaps she is just a stranger whose book he picked up for her – but a book may contain a code or a secret message…

…Snipper opened his eyes and blinked in the glare of her torch.

She pointed it away from him so he could see who it was. He blinked again.

"You!" he snarled.

"You're alive!" she exclaimed.

"Do I disappoint you?" he asked bitterly, staring down the barrel of her gun…

Snipper's journey takes him from the beautiful but dangerous snow-covered slopes of the Altispine Mountains; through the Needlelands where Van Hogloot (a criminal banker with international connections) has his home in a converted windmill; to Icepeak, a remote and starkly beautiful island where Snipper finally comes face-to-face with the mysterious Mr E.

…Their eyes met.

"There will be casualties," said Mr E with a sigh, as though it troubled him a little.

It sent a shiver down Snipper's spines…

Also by Elizabeth Morley

Where Hedgehogs Dare

Where Hedgehogs Dare turns back the clock to the time of Snipper's great-grandmother, Snippette, and the beginning of the Second World War. Great Bristlin stands alone against Hegemony and needs every hedgehog it can get: Spike has joined His Majesty's Air Force and is flying reconnaissance missions; and Clou has formed an escape line to help Bristlish prisoners-of-war on the run.

Snippette is now determined to escape from her enemy-occupied island and do her bit for the war, too – even if it is just making widgets in a factory. However, the mysterious Field Liaison and Espionage Agency (known to its agents as F.L.E.A.) has something altogether more dangerous in mind, and Snippette will soon hold the fate of nations in her paws.

..."Are you afraid to die?" asked the brigadier suddenly.
Snippette thought for a moment. "Yes, sir."
"Then what the blazes makes you think you could work for an organization like F.L.E.A.?"
"Some things are more important than my fear of dying."...

Where Hedgehogs Dare takes Snippette, Flight Lieutenant Spike and Clou, the Comte de Grif, on a dangerous journey through enemy-occupied territory – a parachute drop, crash landing, secret messages, deception and self-sacrifice. Some will be captured. All risk their lives.

...Spike swerved away from the oncoming planes but then others appeared, as if from nowhere. Suddenly they were on his tail...

..."They know what Clou gets up to... if they do capture him, he'll be shot."